HATHOR LEGACY: OUTCAST

Deborah A Bailey

Bright Street Books
PISCATAWAY, NJ

Deborah A Bailey/Bright Street Books™
Piscataway, New Jersey
www.brightstbooks.com

Publisher's Note: This is a work of fiction. Names, characters, places, and incidents are a product of the author's imagination. Locales and public names are sometimes used for atmospheric purposes. Any resemblance to actual people, living or dead, or to businesses, companies, events, institutions, or locales is completely coincidental.

Book Layout ©2013 BookDesignTemplates.com
Cover design by Steph's Cover Design
http://www.stephscoverdesign.com/

Ordering Information:
Quantity sales. Special discounts are available on quantity purchases by corporations, associations, and others. For details, contact the "Sales Department" at the website above.

Hathor Legacy: Outcast/ Deborah A Bailey. -- 1st ed.
ISBN 978-0-9842926-5-3

Acknowledgements

Special thanks to Kelli Wilkins, Kat Duncan, Amy Swencak and my mom, Ruth Bailey for your feedback and support.

"Your real job in the world is to be you."

—India.Arie

1 THE EXPLOSION

Nova City, Hathor - Morning

Nadira was a little girl again, clutching her mother, Minona's hand. As usual, she felt her mother's soft, warm energy flowing through their physical connection. Perched on a mound of thick, steel grey sand, they sat watching the sapphire waves roll up on the shore. Shielding her eyes from the bright sunshine, Nadira watched a bird swoop over the sea, then soar back up into the bright blue sky.

"Mommy, look!" She pointed, directing her mother to follow the bird's progress as it glided above the waves.

Her mother's lips were pressed together in a tight line. Why didn't she smile anymore? What was wrong? Nadira reached up, tracing her mother's full lips with her fingers. Minona smiled, her gold-flecked, brown eyes lighting up at her daughter's touch. But her joy quickly faded.

"They're coming, Nadira."

Now she remembered why they were waiting here on the beach. She wrapped her arms around her mother's neck. Soon the Guardians would come to take her away. Please don't let them take me.

She could hear the aircars approaching, their engines rumbling like thunder. Don't let go, Mommy. Don't let go. As her mother's arms slid around her, Nadira squeezed her tight.

"I love you, Nadira," her mother whispered. "Don't forget."

She wouldn't forget. Never. Determined, she held on to her mother, trying to resist as firm hands grabbed her from behind. But they were too strong for her and yanked her away.

"No!" Nadira sprang up, gasping for breath. Instead of being on a beach with her mother, she was in her apartment in Nova City.

Twenty solar years ago they'd hidden in various seaside towns in the North, eluding the Guardians who relentlessly tracked them. But Nadira's abilities to read people's thoughts and emotions were too strong to remain undetected. When they'd found her, they took her away to be trained as one of them.

If only she and her mother had been able to leave Hathor. But no one with abilities could leave the planet and survive.

Buzzing from the communications unit broke into her musings. Turning off the auto answer had seemed like a good idea last night. Now she'd have to get up and find out who it was.

"Lights up 50%," she called out. Panels of light in the ceiling illuminated the room in a soft white glow.

Nadira threw back the covers. Running her hand over her short-cropped hair, she padded over to get something to put on. On a set of shelves next to the com unit, she kept her company-issued clothing in neatly folded stacks. Grey jackets on top, grey pants below.

Well, at least she had some discretion over the shirt color. Should she choose the off-white or the light grey? Or maybe dark blue?

Buzz--buzz--buzz

Whoever was trying to reach her was not giving up. She pulled out a blue shirt and shrugged it on. Now she was ready.

Her apartment had been built decades before and she'd refused to update any of the built-in appliances-- including the old com unit. Sometimes the video didn't work, other times it was the audio. She tapped the screen. It stayed blank, but she could hear breathing through the tinny speakers.

"Nadira," a man's gruff voice blared. "Do you have the vid turned off again?"

Nothing like getting a call from, Brant, the Guardian Sentry Leader first thing in the morning. "Com unit's acting up."

"Get a new unit."

"We're Guardians, why do we need communicators?" Nadira couldn't resist asking the question. Using their heightened senses, Guardians could connect with each other without using man-made devices. Though communicating with Brant wasn't something she looked forward to.

There was silence, followed by a sigh. "We have an alert about an explosion and theft at the mine on Demeter. Several workers were killed."

It was the highest-producing mine in the solar system, just three days away by interplanetary shuttle. Lots of security. Hard to believe someone from the outside would try to steal from it. "How did they get through the checkpoints?"

"They were probably helped by someone on the inside. The CEO of the mine is missing along with a sizable amount of crystal. He might be involved."

"But what can the Guardians do about it?" she asked. The mine had its own security force. Besides, she was here on Hathor, what could she do? As a Sentry she had the strongest abilities of all the Guardians.

But still, she didn't have the power to do anything about a theft millions of kilometers away.

"We do not ignore direct requests from Novacorp. If the thieves come here, we must apprehend them. I don't need to remind you of your duty, do I? We Guardians are responsible for protecting this planet."

And now he was going into one of his long-winded speeches. Hadn't she always done her duty? Even after being taken from her mother she'd served Novacorp. For years she'd turned her back on her own desires to do what they wanted.

"But why would they risk coming here?" Novacorp's headquarters was here on Hathor.

"They risked stealing from the mine, they might risk much more. Novacorp knows best and we will follow their directives. Do you understand?" His tone cut off further discussion.

Of course she did. It had been drilled into her since she was eight years old: the age she'd been taken from her mother.

"Yes, I understand," Nadira replied. Please let this conversation be over now.

"I will contact you later with further instructions."

"Fine." She punched the com unit and disconnected. Their calls usually ended this way.

After dealing with the Sentry Leader, she was in no mood to go back to bed. Brant was prone to exaggerate, but he might be right this time.

If the thieves were coming to Hathor, it would be up to the Guardians to stop them.

Mining Port City, Astarte - Morning

"Jonathan! Come here, Jon!"

Half asleep, Jonathan responded to his father's voice. "I'll be right there."

Might as well get up and see what his father wanted--wait a minute. Jon slowly opened his eyes, surveying his surroundings. He was in his bed alone. Or was he? Out of the corner of his eye he made out a cloud of bright red hair and the curve of a feminine shoulder. What was her name again? Lina...no, it was Lela. That's right. Lela something or other.

His father's voice had been so clear. Great. Now he was hearing things that weren't there. Jon burrowed deeper into his pillow. But what did he expect after only a couple of hours sleep? The party he'd hosted last night had gone on into the early hours of the morning.

Easing his hand out from under the covers, he tapped on the surface of the bedside table. Might as well check out the news alerts. The wall in front of him glowed blue before it displayed the attractive face of a woman with short brown hair. Not wanting to wake his companion, he kept the sound low.

Now they were showing the mining installation on the neighboring moon, Demeter. He hadn't been there in months. And when he'd gone it was only because his father, the mine CEO, had asked him to come. Jonathan had given in to his father's request. Unfortunately, he'd been unable to fake an interest in his father's work.

Suddenly the bottom of the screen was flashing red, accompanied by scenes of wrecked equipment and caved in mineshafts. What the hell? He turned up the volume in time to hear the words: "blast," "accident," "killed." Mining officials were being interviewed. Jonathan jumped out of bed and ran into the main living area. Was his father supposed to be at the mine today?

He picked up his tablet, his hand shaking. "Contact Brandon Keel on Demeter."

A moment later the long, tired face of a man he didn't recognize filled the screen. He frowned like he'd just smelled something sour. "Demeter mining installation 12-100--CEO's office."

"Where is he? Put him on."

"Who is this?"

"His son, Jonathan. Who are you?"

Jon heard someone talking in the background. The man got up, and his father's second-in-command, Catherine Mantee sat down. "Jonathan, there's no need to worry."

"Cat! Where's my father?" He noticed she was paler than usual, and her blue eyes were bloodshot.

"We don't know yet. Brandon told me he was leaving on the shuttle for Hathor this morning." She sighed, absently rubbing her forehead. "We're trying to contact him now."

"What caused the explosion?"

"We're not sure. But it looks like it was a diversion to cover the theft. Look, we'll know more in a few hours," she answered in a shaky voice.

"A theft? Then it wasn't an accident? I'll be there as soon as I can to help look for my father."

"No, Jonathan! We're still picking up the pieces here."

"But my father is missing." Jon ran his fingers through his hair, but couldn't keep a curl from falling back against his forehead. "You can't expect me just to wait here and do nothing."

"You can't get here. Company and private shuttles are on lockdown. I've given the order. No one is coming or going right now."

"I have to do something." He paced the floor, his feet slapping the stone tiles. "You have to find him."

"Jonathan, I swear we will." More muffled voices in the background. Cat's frown deepened. "There was another cave in. I've got to go."

"What about my father? Cat, what's going on?"

The screen went blank.

2 DEEPER AND DEEPER

In spite of his misgivings after his conversation with Cat, Jonathan went to his club that evening. With a little help from his father, he'd bought an old warehouse by the shuttle station and turned it into a popular venue.

Naming it, "The Answer," he'd opened the club expecting it to be a success. And it was. There was nowhere else in the city where everyone could come together to dance, drink and do whatever they desired.

Taking up his usual position in a private lounge overlooking the dance floor, he scanned the crowd. From the looks of things, it was going to be another busy night.

On the level below, the floor was packed with bodies writhing to the thumping beat. Multicolored lights flashed, illuminating the darkened space at timed intervals. The occupancy was limited to 500, and he was sure they'd have to close the doors soon. It wasn't unusual for lines to form outside, which only added to the exclusivity.

Behind him he heard the clink of glasses and laughter as a few of his regular guests relaxed on the plush couches. It was time to join them and try to be a good host.

Damn it. Cat should've gotten back to him by now. What was taking her so long? Forcing a smile to his lips, he acknowledged one of his patrons as she waved to him from the dance floor.

"I didn't think you'd be here tonight," a voice purred behind him.

Jon spun around. He looked into the dark eyes of a woman wearing a black tank top and pants that looked like they'd been painted onto her shapely body.

"Ilana. Where have you been?" Jon drew her into his arms, taking in her spicy perfume. Every time he saw her, her hair was a different color and length. Now it was black and cropped short, barely touching the bottom of her ears. His eyes were drawn to dangling crystal earrings hanging down to her bare, creamy shoulders.

"I had business to take care of. Sorry I didn't tell you I was leaving last time," She raked her hands across his back. "I heard about the explosion at the mine. Is it true your father is missing?"

"He left for Hathor before the blast. We haven't heard from him yet." He led her over to a couch at the rear of the lounge. "But I'm sure he'll contact us when he gets in."

"Of course he will." Ilana whispered in his ear, her fingertips playing over the growing bulge in his pants. "You know, Jon. There's something I've always wondered. Why did you call your club, 'The Answer?'"

Jon shuddered as she continued to tease him. "It's a private joke."

"You won't tell me? There shouldn't be any secrets between us."

"It's got nothing to do with us." Between her scent and what she was doing to him with her fingers, he was aching. But as he was about to reach over and do some teasing of his own, she abruptly pulled out of his grasp.

"Is that how you're going to treat me? I was going to tell you something. Now I don't know if I should," she said, her voice trembling.

"What is it?"

"When I was coming back on the shuttle from Hathor a couple of days ago, I overheard a man and woman talking. They were saying things about the mine and they mentioned your father's name a lot." Her dark brown eyes filled with alarm. "I don't think

they were business people, Jon. They sounded dangerous."

"Did you get a look at them?"

Ilana shook her head. "I only heard them talking."

"We'll tell Cat to check this out. She'll want to
question them."

"Cat?" Ilana asked.

"Catherine Mantee. She's Chief of Security at the
mine."

"Oh no, I can't." Ilana's eyes filled with tears. "Suppose they come after me?"

Now he'd done it. Jonathan wrapped his arms
around her, gently patting her shoulder. "It's okay.
Don't worry. I'll tell Cat myself."

"I'm so sorry, Jon. I wish I could be more helpful."
She eased herself out of his embrace. "I have to go. Do
you mind?"

"What? You just got here."

"I'll see you later. I promise." She got up and rushed
towards the stairs.

"Wait, Ilana!" He reached the stairway in time to
see her disappear into the crowd below.

Now what? Well, at least he had a lead on the
thieves. Cat would have to follow it up. If she didn't,
he'd handle it himself.

Two days later Jonathan wasn't any closer to getting answers. Even offering payment for information

had led him nowhere. And to make things worse, Cat had refused to believe Ilana's story.

Disgusted and tired of the gossip from his friends about his father and the theft, he left the club early and headed home. Friends? Sure they were, as long as he paid for the entertainment.

In the meantime, Ilana hadn't turned up again. Not that it was surprising. Appearing and disappearing unexpectedly was the norm for her. But as frustrating as it was, it always left him desperate to see her again.

What was surprising was to find her huddled in his doorway when he got back to his apartment. As soon as she saw him, she launched herself into his arms.

"Ilana! What's going on?"

"They're after me! We have to get inside."

He touched the fingerpad on his front door, identifying himself to the security system. As the door swung open, he cast a wary glance behind him before helping her inside.

Under the brighter lights of the foyer, he took a good look at her. Dark smears of eye makeup streaked her face, making her skin look ashen. When he released her, he saw that her short silver jacket was ripped at the shoulder.

"Ilana, what happened?" He guided her to one the couches in the living area. "Are you all right?"

She nodded. "A man chased me when I was leaving the transport station. He grabbed me, but I was able to get free. I ran all the way here."

"We'll have to contact mine security."

"No, Jon! I--I think I know who it was. The other night after I went back to my place, I had a message. A woman told me to leave Astarte as soon as possible."

"Why didn't you call me?"

Ilana managed to stop sobbing long enough to answer him. "I don't know. But I recognized the voice, Jon. It was the woman from the shuttle. They know I overheard them."

"But how could they?" Jon asked.

"I don't know how!" Ilana leapt up and paced the room. "Maybe it's because you've been asking around. They must be getting nervous. Jon, I've got to leave this planet."

"We need to report this." He stood and put his arms around her. "Mine security can protect you."

"For all you know, those people killed your father. I'm leaving as soon as I can. I need shuttle passes and security clearance to get to Hathor. Can you help me?"

"What about the company you work for? Can't they get you passes to go back?"

"My trip here wasn't for business, Jon. I came just to see you. The mine put extra security in place after the theft. Suppose they stop me? If I can't leave, those people will come after me." Trembling, she started crying again. "Please, Jonathan. I want to get back to Hathor."

All this time he'd been hoping to persuade her to talk to Cat directly. But the shape she was in, it wasn't going to happen. Helping her to leave Astarte was the only way to be sure she'd be safe.

"Don't cry. I'll get you on a shuttle."

Gripping him tight, she whispered in his ear, her warm breath tickling him. "I knew you could help."

The buzzer sounded. What the hell? He wasn't expecting visitors.

"Go into the bedroom, close the door and stay there." He waited for her to head into his room. After he heard the door click shut, he strode over to check the security monitor. Cat's face stared back at him. Now this was unexpected.

"Jonathan." Cat gave him a quick smile as she entered. "We've got to talk." She took off her black company-issued jacket and slung it over her shoulder.

"You have news about my father?" Jon asked.

"Got anything in your bar?" She gestured towards a set of glass shelves along the opposite wall. Lined up on them was an assortment of liquors, most of them souvenirs of his father's travels.

"What do you want?"

"You still have your father's Scotch?" she asked.

"Sure."

Brandon had gotten it during one of his infrequent trips back to the Earth system. Jonathan poured the amber liquid into a glass and handed it to her. He noticed she'd practically finished it before he'd poured his own drink. By the time he settled down on the couch across from her, her glass was empty.

"You want more?" he asked.

"No. I couldn't handle another one." Cat set the glass down on the table in front of her. "Look. I'm going to get to the point. You're interfering with our investigation."

"I'm trying to find out what happened to my father. What are you doing about it?"

Cat stiffened. "Brandon's also my friend. Besides, I told you he left for Hathor."

"Then why haven't we heard from him by now? You can't stop me. If that's why you came, you can leave now." He hoped the authority in his voice would sway her, but her expression didn't change.

"As Mine Security Chief I can stop anything I choose." Cat pointed towards a hunk of golden brown crystal sitting on a shelf above the bottled liquors. "I was with your father when he found that. When he showed it to me, I told him it was the most beautiful crystal I'd ever seen. And, believe me, Brandon and I found a lot of them."

Jonathan sighed. He'd heard this story before. All about the old days before his father and mother had met. Brandon and Cat had been freelancers working in one of the mining installations on Hathor. Eventually they joined Novacorp and took over the mine on Demeter, making it the most profitable one in the system.

But he knew her reason for bringing up the past. It was the same reason she always brought it up. Cat had known his father long before he, his mother and his sisters were in Brandon's life. She wanted to remind Jonathan who had been there first.

"I do have news. The security monitor replay showed your father walking with a woman about an hour before the explosion," Cat said. "He was probably on his way to the shuttle."

"Do you know who she is?"

"Couldn't see her face. We were able to track her up to the explosion. Afterwards the monitor malfunctioned."

"It must've been the woman I told you about. Was there a man with her?"

"Jonathan, there was no couple on the shuttle plotting to steal from the mine. That friend of yours is lying." Cat looked away for a moment. "But, there's something I didn't tell you."

"What is it?"

"They found the Ops Director a few hours ago. His body was thrown into one of the shafts in Sector 8. Not far from where your father was seen with the woman."

Jon's heart thundered in his chest. For all he knew, his father could be at the bottom of a mineshaft right now. Or maybe he did go to Hathor. There had to be a way to find out.

"If you can't confirm my father was on the shuttle, your investigation skills aren't worth a damn." Jonathan headed back to the bar to pour another drink. But his attempt at staying cool wasn't working. His hand shook so much that half his drink splashed onto the countertop.

"Look, I need you to stop causing trouble and trust me. All you need to know is that your father left for Hathor." She stood up and grabbed her jacket. "Let me handle this."

"Sure." He gulped his drink down, refusing to make eye contact with her. The next thing he heard was her footfall across the floor. The door opened and closed, followed by silence.

After resetting the door to lock, Jon sprinted back to his room. When he entered, Ilana was sitting on the bed examining his tablet. Startled, she dropped the device. Jon picked it up. Luckily it hadn't broken when it hit the stone floor.

"Were you looking for something?" he asked, as he sat down next to her.

"I was checking the shuttle schedule. There's one leaving tomorrow. Who was that?"

"Cat. A security monitor showed my father walking with a woman before the explosion."

"Did they really see her on the monitor?"

"They couldn't identify her." Jonathan expected Ilana to be relieved, but she started crying again. "What is it?"

"Please, Jonathan. You have to help me leave." She clutched his shirt, her nails digging into his chest. "Why don't you come with me to Hathor? I could help you look for your father there."

"I don't know. What if these people go after my family?"

"Jon, your family is wealthy. You can hire a team of security guards to protect them. Will you get the passes? Can we leave together?"

"Yes, Ilana. I'll get them. We'll leave on the next shuttle."

Much later in the evening Jonathan headed over to see his mother, Estrella. Taking an aircar there was the quickest way, compared to spending an hour travelling in a ground vehicle.

After the aircar set down on the pad, Jonathan instructed the driver to wait for him. It was a clear night, the sky filled with countless stars and Demeter shining bright enough to illuminate his surroundings.

As he approached, he could see activity inside the house. Not that it was difficult with the glass wall encasing the lower level.

"Jonathan." His mother came over to embrace him as he entered the foyer. Dressed in a flowing, sleeveless dress, she gathered her brown hair off her shoulders and twisted it into a knot. "I thought you were coming out tomorrow."

"Are the girls here?" His sisters, Verda and Brisa were 17 and 21, and as far as they were concerned, far from being girls. In fact, he only called them that to tease them, which they usually didn't appreciate.

"Upstairs. Why? Is something wrong?"

"Let's go where we won't be interrupted."

Estrella's grey eyes, the same color as his own, grew wide as she reacted to his words.

"Why can't they hear what you have to say?" she asked.

"I don't want to worry them. Please, it's important we talk."

Instead of questioning him further, she led him to her suite in the rear of the house. Once they were inside, she closed the door and sat in her usual chair by the window.

Jon remembered many nights he'd sat there with her as she told him stories about her life on Hathor. She and his grandparents lived in a place called the West Country. And they'd had a farm, or was it a ranch? He couldn't remember.

The back of the house faced the ocean, and it was quiet enough to hear the waves crashing against the rocks below.

"Have you heard from Dad?"

Estrella's gaze penetrated him like she could see what he was thinking. It seemed strange, but when she looked at him that way, he wondered if she really could read his thoughts.

"Not yet, but Brandon said he was going to Hathor."

"But he should've arrived by now. Aren't you concerned?"

"No, I'm not, Jon," she said, her voice steady.

"I've heard rumors that he was involved in the theft."

"Jon, I don't care what people think. Your father didn't do it." In spite of her sharp words, there was no anger in her tone or expression. She never spoke to him in anger, but her calm could be much more intimidating.

"I met someone who overheard the thieves. She's in danger and needs my help," he blurted out.

"Who is this person?"

"I'd rather not say."

"Jon, what are you about to do?"

"If anyone asks, just say I went to Hathor on business."

"I don't want you to go." Estrella came to her feet, her hands balled into fists. "We'll find your father, I'm certain of it. It's not safe for you there."

"Why not? You were born there. It'll be like going back home." He smiled, hoping to diffuse her fears. "Why don't you want me to go?"

"Just promise me you won't go."

"When I get there I'll go to company security and ask them to take over the investigation. Don't worry. I'll be back in a few days."

He gathered her into his arms. Usually his mother didn't like a lot of hugging and touching. She'd shown affection to him and his sisters in many ways, but physical closeness like this was rare for her.

"Please don't worry. I won't be in danger," he whispered. He couldn't lie to her. But he could tell her what he knew she needed to hear.

"Whatever happens, Jonathan, you must never tell anyone that I'm from Hathor. Do you promise? Say nothing."

"Why not?"

"Promise me." She gripped him, her fingers digging into his flesh.

"I promise, Mother. I won't tell anyone."

3 THIEVES LIKE US

Astarte - Morning

Using his father's security clearance, it hadn't been difficult for Jonathan to get the shuttle passes for himself and Ilana. But just to be on the safe side, she suggested he use an alias when getting her passes. That way, no one would know she was on her way to Hathor.

Another advantage of using Brandon's clearance was that they didn't have to go through security checkpoints. The shuttle to Hathor was usually filled with Novacorp managers and other company workers. Just the group of passengers to mix in with if you didn't want to be subjected to a lot of scrutiny.

Other than Estrella, the only person who knew Jonathan was leaving was his assistant at the club. Not only was she very capable, but she was good at keeping confidences. He'd only be gone for a week or so. She'd have no problem handling things until he got back.

Cat would be pissed if she checked the passenger lists and saw his name. Thinking of it made him smile. He didn't need her approval to look for his father.

Once they were onboard, Jonathan led the way to the private suites. An attendant showed them to their room and left them to settle in. Though it was compact, it included a bed large enough for them both. There was even room for a narrow table and two chairs.

Jon dropped his bag and settled down on the bed.

"Jonathan." Ilana plopped down next to him. "Aren't you glad you got one of the executive suites? I told you it would be more comfortable."

He rested against the pillows. "You were right."

Sure, it was comfortable. But one of the basic rooms would've been fine. Why had he let himself be talked into reserving this one? But, maybe she was right. At least they wouldn't be crammed into bunk beds with no room to move around.

"I wish I could've gone back to my place to get my clothing." Ilana pulled off her torn jacket and threw it on the bed. "I must look terrible."

"I'll buy you clothing when we get in." Jon drew her into a kiss.

Ilana playfully bit his lip. "We have three days, Jon. I'm hungry. I've always wanted to try the gourmet menu."

The engines started up, sending a vibration through the bed, followed by the ding of a warning bell. The door was closing.

In a few moments they'd be shooting out into space. Now he could relax and enjoy three days with Ilana in a private suite. Things could definitely be worse.

Hathor - Late afternoon

It wasn't often that Nadira was called to her mentor, Zina's apartment for a private meeting. But Zina wanted to discuss the theft on Demeter without having to involve Brant or any of the other Guardians.

Riding in the ground transport vehicle, Nadira studied the people strolling down the boulevard. Zina's apartment was in the wealthiest part of the city, called the Palatine. It was filled with shops and restaurants catering to the executives and other powerful residents.

The transport pulled out of the traffic lanes and came to a stop in front of an amber-colored apartment tower. Nadira stepped out onto the shiny marble sidewalk, scanning the pedestrians passing in front of the tower entrance. Two men walked past wearing the dark brown suits popular with company executives. A city security officer went by in the opposite direction, wearing a black one-piece uniform and shiny helmet.

Nadira was about to walk into the building when she felt it. A stirring within her that grew stronger. Glancing to her left, she saw a tall, thin man with long black hair walking towards her, his glittering green jacket flapping as he moved. He stopped at a shop next to the building, and entered.

At the shop window she had a clear view of what was going on inside. A man and woman were looking at a necklace the shopkeeper was holding. The long-haired man stood opposite them, his back turned. He picked up one of the large green crystals from a display, examined it, and slid it into his jacket pocket.

It was bold to steal from a shop in the Palatine. City security regularly patrolled the area. Should she go back and alert the officer? No, Hathor was her home. He was a thief and she had a duty to stop him.

Nadira entered the stop and stood by the door. Now he was examining a yellow stone between his thumb and forefinger, holding it up to catch the light of the late afternoon sun.

She held up her left hand to identify herself to the shopkeeper, showing him the half-moon line that had formed in her palm after she'd developed her Guardian abilities.

Behind the glass-topped counter, the shopkeeper stared at her, open-mouthed. His customers were transfixed as well. Nadira waited as the thief slowly turned to look at her out of the corner of his eye.

Redness spread up the man's neck and across the side of his face, like a rash. She took a step forward. The crystal he was holding fell from his hand and bounced along the carpeted floor.

He reached under his jacket, pulling out a small oval-shaped object. A stunner. If she gave him time, he'd use the weapon against her and the others in the shop. Taking in a deep breath, Nadira summoned up her energy. It surged from deep within her, rushing through her body like a wave.

Now her heart was pounding faster and faster, the beats vibrating in her ears. She reached out and sent a blast of energy in his direction.

He fell back against the jewelry display, knocking down the glass shelves and sending crystals flying across the shop. Dropping to his knees, he clutched at his stomach and cried out.

"AGGGGH!"

Though she was more powerful than most Guardians, her stronger abilities required her to have stronger skills. She had to be careful not to use too much power when confronting a target.

Being hit by an energy blast was similar to experiencing an electrical shock. Sending out more power could disable or even kill. But she'd been trained to use her abilities only to defend--never to attack--unless she had a reason.

On his knees now the thief reached out, attempting to grab her leg. Dodging out of his grasp, she avoided him. Groaning, he fell flat on the floor, his face down against the carpet.

Zina had taught her to remain distant from her work, to do what needed to be done with no emotion. For the most part she was able to follow that directive. But at times it was difficult to watch someone suffer and know that she was the cause of it.

"Guardian--thank the stars!" The shopkeeper rushed over to her, mopping his fleshy face with the back of his hand.

"Don't you have a security guard standing by?" she asked.

"I sent her to my other store to retrieve an item," he replied, prodding the unconscious thief with the toe of his shoe. "What about this slag?"

"Contact city security to take him to detention. I'll wait."

Continuing to wipe the sweat off his brow, he bowed and hurried to the rear of the shop. The couple he'd been helping took turns staring at her and at the man lying at her feet. She'd seen that look before, a mixture of awe and apprehension. Almost in unison they backed away from the jewelry display, whispering to each other.

"That's a Guardian? She looks like everyone else. What did she do to him?"

"Shhh--don't say anything," the man replied.

Moments later, two city security officers burst into the shop, grabbed the thief and hoisted him to his feet. Groggy and mumbling to himself, he stumbled as they dragged him out of the store.

Stopping the man hadn't taken much effort. Even though her hands were trembling, the confrontation had barely tired her. Her heart rate would be back to normal soon. And once she regained her full strength the trembling would go away too.

Nadira stood by the window watching the officers push the thief into a waiting vehicle before climbing in. Behind them, the thick metal door slid into place with a loud clang.

4 Lost and Found

Three Days Later - On the Shuttle to Hathor

Jonathan spent most of the trip planning what he and Ilana would do when they docked on Hathor. At least they had recycled water for showering instead of the waterless soap passengers in the basic rooms had to use. When he stepped out of the shower, Ilana was already dressed and sitting on the end of the bed.

"Are you in a hurry?" he asked.

"I think we should go to the hotel separately."

"Why?" He sat down next to her.

"Just in case we're being followed."

"That doesn't make sense. We should stay together."

"Jon..." Ilana tugged at the towel he'd hitched around his waist. It came loose and she reached under the folds. "We've had so much fun together and we'll have more when we get to the hotel."

He tensed as she aroused him to the point of exploding. Damn. If only they had more time.

Ilana trailed her hand across his thigh. "Haven't you had enough?"

"No," Jonathan said, leaning her down across the bed.

The warning buzzer sounded. They'd be docking very soon.

"Jonathan." Ilana slid out from his grasp with more force than he'd expected. "There's no time for that now. We've got to get out of here."

He got up and reached for the towel. When he looked over, Ilana was turned away from him, putting on her jacket. Might as well get dressed.

After they docked, the warning bell sounded and the engines powered down. Occupied with throwing his clothes into his bag, Jonathan didn't notice Ilana heading out the door.

"Ilana! Wait!" Grabbing his things, he raced after her.

Passengers clogged the aisle before he could get to the exit. He'd been locked away for so long that he'd almost forgotten there were over 100 people on the shuttle. And it seemed like all of them wanted to get to the door at the same time.

Pushing past the slower travelers, he got a glimpse of Ilana on the exit ramp. Luckily, her silver jacket made her stand out. In front of him was a sea of people in grey and brown suits and the occasional person dressed in dark blue mining overalls. Black-garbed security officers stood off to the side, their faces covered by shiny helmets.

The ramp opened up into the main concourse of the terminal. Advertising vids flashed on the walls, while announcements blared from the loudspeakers.

"Nova City Entertainments announces the grand opening of their complex for executive-level luxury."

"Visit the brand new Galaxy dance club tonight and receive an exclusive--"

"--our newest apartment tower, now open for rentals at the city's most exclusive address--"

All around him people were rushing in what seemed like a hundred different directions. Holographic signs displayed the arrivals and departures, while news alerts were being broadcast on floor to ceiling glass panels. Bright sunlight poured through the arched, glass ceiling and reflected off the jewel-toned walls, creating the illusion the floor was covered with precious gems.

For a moment he didn't know where he was going. People knocked into him, almost turning him around in their hurry to get past. Damn it. He had to get it together. Scanning his surroundings, he saw an exit sign ahead. Maybe he could catch up with Ilana before she got outside.

Quickening his pace, he dodged the oncoming foot traffic and a few automated luggage carts. Just before he got to the exit doors, he saw Ilana standing in front of a lift. Breaking into a run he called out to her.

"Ilana! Wait up!"

When the lift doors opened, she turned and their eyes met.

"Ilana!"

Instead of responding, she ran inside and stood in the rear, her arms crossed.

Wait!" A luggage cart zoomed in front of him, forcing him to stop short before he barged into it. Pushing it away, he picked up the pace again. He'd hitched his travel bag across his body, and it banged against his back as he ran.

Just as he got to the lift, it closed in his face. Slamming his hand against the metal door, he waited for it to slide open again. But it didn't.

"Damn it!" What the hell was Ilana thinking? He was trying to help her.

"Jonathan. What's wrong with you?" A man's deep voice boomed from behind him. "I've been chasing you across the place."

Spinning around, he faced a slightly taller, older man with straight, steel-grey hair that fell to his shoulders. He wore a dark purple jacket, trimmed with gold and dark grey pants. On his fingers were gold and silver rings that glistened as he gestured.

"Matt!" Jonathan relaxed as he was pulled into the older man's embrace. "What are you doing here?"

Matt grinned, grasping Jonathan's shoulder with a hearty shake. "Your mother sent me a message. She told me you were coming in. How the hell are you?"

Jon hadn't thought of contacting his father's friend. But of course his mother had. It had been several years since they'd seen each other in person.

There were a few more wrinkles around his brown eyes and across his forehead than Jon remembered. But being out of the mines, and spending more time outdoors, had given Matt's face a suntanned glow. An improvement over the pallor a lot of miners developed after years of working in the caverns, no matter what their skin tone.

"Who were you running after?" Matt led the way towards a row of glass doors.

"Just someone I met on the shuttle," Jonathan replied. "Still got the club?"

"Sure. It's doing great. It's a private club for executives, you know. Didn't your father tell you? He was here on business a few months ago."

"No, he didn't mention that. Have you heard from him lately? Mother said he was supposed to come back to Hathor."

"Brandon didn't say anything about coming back here," Matt said, as they exited into the bright sunlight. "Is Estrella doing okay? She's not worried, is she?"

"No. She's fine," Jonathan replied.

"I couldn't believe it when I heard about the explosion." Matt's voice was quiet. "What's going on with the investigation?"

"I'm trying to figure that out." Jon debated telling his father's friend exactly why he'd come. But he didn't want to share what Ilana had overheard. Better to not involve Matt and endanger him as well.

"We'll get a transport to my place," Matt said. "I've got lots of room."

"I've got reservations at the Emerald Club. Can you drop me off?"

"Sure...if you want."

"Thanks for the offer. But I'm meeting someone later."

They walked over to a row of ground transports parked at the curb. As Matt approached the first one, a shiny, ruby-colored model, the door slid back. Jon climbed in after him and settled himself on the long, cushioned seat.

"Emerald Club," Matt instructed the autodriver.

The engines powered up with a low hum, then the vehicle pulled away from the curb and into the traffic lanes.

Matt put his feet up on the seat opposite them. "I heard the company is investigating the explosion like it's an inside job."

"Do you think my father was involved?" Jonathan asked.

"Hell, no. Your father's my oldest friend. He had nothing to do with this. Just telling you what I heard."

"Sure."

"Back when I was in the mines, they had lots of explosions from sabotage, disgruntled workers, stupid asses who didn't know what they're doing--shit happens all the time." Matt shook his head, his hair falling across his shoulders. "Saw a lot of it when I worked with your father."

"Hey, didn't you have the tats last time I saw you?" Jonathan pointed to Matt's bare wrists. Resembling dark red tongues of flame, the tats were applied to a miner's wrists once they signed on with Novacorp. They were encoded with the miner's ID and made it easier to track them when they worked at the various company installations.

"I had them removed." Matt absently rubbed his wrist as he stared straight ahead. "I'm a businessman now, not a laborer." He pointed over to a building they were passing on the right. "Look over there. I just invested in it. It's a new exclusive apartment tower. A couple of months ago I got a big house out in the North overlooking the sea. If you'll be here for a while, I'll take you to see it."

"You have lots of credits to spend."

"That's why I'm here. Brandon's got a good position, but he'd be wealthier if he'd stayed here on Hathor. Do you still have your club? Your father hoped having a business would keep you out of trouble."

"It doesn't." Jonathan grinned.

"You're just like me, Jonathan." Matt laughed. "Who the hell wants a quiet life? I'd rather be here in the heart of everything."

"My mother thinks I'm in danger. You know what that's about?"

"She's a mother." Matt looked down and picked at bits of lint on his pants. "She wants to keep you safe."

"So all these people live here?" Jon asked as he watched the crowds filling the streets. Even the transport traffic lanes were clogged with vehicles, slowly trundling down the boulevard.

"On Hathor, you're either connected to Novacorp or you're a civilian," Matt said. "Or, you're one of the Guardians."

Jonathan tensed. "They really exist? I thought those were stories."

"They exist. They're descendants of the original settled who came here generations ago. Even before Novacorp was here." Matt patted Jonathan's shoulder. "They're more powerful than company security. Some of them can even read what you're thinking. But as long as you stay out of trouble, they won't bother you."

Twenty minutes later, the transport dropped Jonathan off in front of the Emerald Club, a thirty-story building that resembled layers of glittering green glass. Striding across the gleaming marbled sidewalk, he passed a row of gold, manicured trees lining the entrance.

The glass doors swooped open to admit him to a gold-toned marble lobby. An attendant dressed in a dark green jacket and pants took his bag and led him to a private alcove.

"Mr. Keel," the bald man motioned to an ornately carved chair. "My name is Mr. Renard. Please have a seat and we'll take care of everything."

"Did my guest arrive yet?" Jon asked.

"Um...no...no one else has arrived in your party. May I verify the name?"

"Cintra Ansi."

"No, she hasn't arrived. When do you expect her?"

"I thought she'd be here. We just got in on the shuttle."

"Oh yes." The attendant touched the glass tabletop with his fingertip. Jon couldn't get a good look at what was being displayed there, but he could tell from Mr. Renard's quizzical expression that something was wrong.

"There's a slight problem, Mr. Keel. You made the reservation through Brandon Keel's company account?"

"Yes." Jon shifted in his chair. "He's my father and the CEO of the mine on Demeter."

"I'm sorry, but your father's account has been locked."

"What?"

"It says here," the attendant replied as he pointed to the display, "that the CEO's account was locked this morning."

"Who did it?"

"It's by order of Demeter Mine Security. There is no explanation," Mr. Renard replied, a look of discomfort on his face. "Is there another account that you would like to use?"

Jonathan grabbed his bag and dug through it, buying a few moments to think. Mine Security? It had to be Cat. Damn.

He could use his own account to check in. But what if security was alerted when he used his ID? He was being paranoid again, wasn't he?

"I'll check in later," Jon said. "If my guest arrives before I get back, ask her to wait here."

"Yes, of course," Mr. Renard replied.

Jonathan barely waited for the doors to open before he hurried outside. Where would he go now? He could call Matt and stay at his place. He spotted an information kiosk at the corner. Perfect. It should be easy to find Matt in the directory and get the location of his apartment.

"Mr. Keel."

Startled, Jon stopped short. Turning to his left he looked into the blue eyes of a woman dressed in a smoky grey uniform. Perhaps he hadn't been so paranoid after all. "Yes?"

She managed a tight smile. "Lieutenant Kira, Novacorp Security." She patted a row of four small crystals on her jacket collar. "Please accompany me to the Novacorp Administration building. We have a few questions for you," she said, her voice monotone.

"Is this about the account?" he asked.

"They're waiting for you. You must come with me now."

5 QUESTIONS

Thirty minutes later, Lt. Kira led Jon to an empty office in the Novacorp Administration building. After she left, he sat down in front of a long glass-topped table. A row of windows along the left side of the room faced the dark grey wall of another building.

When the door opened, a man and woman walked in, both dressed in smoky grey suits. The man, rounder and heavier, sat down at the desk.

The woman remained by the door, her arms folded across her chest. Her short dark hair was combed back flat against her head, revealing a rounded and attractive face. Unfortunately her suit didn't allow Jonathan to see very much of her body.

"Mr. Keel, my name is Brant. I'm the Guardian Sentry Chief." Brant's brown bushy eyebrows moved up and down as he spoke. "I will be leading your questioning."

"You're the what?" Jon hadn't heard that title before. But Novacorp was filled with bureaucrats.

"The Sentry Leader, Mr. Keel." Brant pressed his palm against the desktop, causing one of the window panels to become opaque.

"Why am I here?" As he watched, Jonathan saw his name and picture scrolling down the panel. Followed by other stats including the property he owned, the name and location of his club and his father's name and title.

What he didn't see was his mother or sisters mentioned. But he knew better than to bring it up. No need to volunteer any information.

"You own a club in the Astarte port city called, "The Answer." You're 32 years old. Height 190.5 centimeters. Born on Astarte. Birth mother not noted. No contracted partner." Brant read off the details with no emotion, his finger swiping over the desktop.

"Your father, Brandon Keel is the CEO of the mine where the property destruction and robbery occurred. No contracted partner. He is still unaccounted for," Brant continued.

"That can't be right. My father left for Hathor before the theft. He should've arrived days ago."

"There is no record of his arrival, Mr. Keel." The Sentry Leader kept his attention on the display. "You must have been given incorrect information."

It had to be a mistake. "Look. I came to Hathor to talk to security. I know someone who has information about the theft. Let's talk to them and get this cleared up."

No one said anything. Out of the corner of his eye, Jonathan noticed the woman shifting her body. He could feel her staring at him.

"You arrived on the shuttle from Astarte with someone who calls herself, Cintra Ansi," Brant said, ignoring Jon's statement. "Where is she now?"

"That's what I'm saying. I brought her here because the thieves were after her. But we got separated at the terminal."

The Sentry Leader's bland expression didn't change. "Are you contracted with her?" he asked.

"Contracted? With Cin--I mean, with her? No, I'm not. I know her from my club. She saw the people who did the robbery. They threatened her."

Brant nodded, glancing over at the woman. Instead of acknowledging him, she continued to stare at Jonathan.

"When did she see them?" The Sentry Leader touched the desktop again and Jonathan's information disappeared.

"She was traveling from Hathor to Astarte and she overheard them on the shuttle."

"I see." Brant came to his feet and clasped his hands behind him. "And you don't know where she is?"

"No, I don't." Jonathan looked at the woman. Why was she looking at him like that? "You have to find her. She needs protection."

"Mr. Keel, do you know that her name is not Cintra Ansi?"

"We used an alias in case the thieves tried to track her."

Brant looked over at the woman again. This time she nodded.

"Mr. Keel, Cintra Ansi was the name of the Operations Director at mining installation 103-44. Her body was found in one of the mineshafts two months ago." He leaned across the desk. "The woman who entered Hathor with you is called Ilana Travac, a suspect in Ansi's disappearance."

"You're wrong!" No way could Ilana do anything like that.

"You were deceived by this person, Mr. Keel. If she's responsible for Cintra Ansi's death, she may be responsible for your father's disappearance as well."

"I know her. She came to me for help. Why aren't you looking for the people who did this? Or are you questioning me to cover your incompetence?"

Brant's face twisted into frown. "Mr. Keel, perhaps your involvement in this should be investigated further. I--"

A loud buzz interrupted him. Brant motioned for the woman to approach. They spoke quietly, then he left the room.

"What the hell is going on?" Jon asked. "Who are you?"

"My name is Nadira and you are talking to a Guardian. Does that answer your question?" She came over and sat on the edge of the desk.

Jonathan stood so that he wouldn't have to look up at her. "I'm a private citizen, not a criminal."

"Then why did you use the CEO's clearance to get passes to travel here?" she asked. "That sounds like something a thief would do."

"Are you a Guardian or an accountant?"

Nadira pursed her lips. He was starting to enjoy this. Why should he be the only one who was pissed off? But now that she was closer, he could get a better view.

Appraising her, he noticed that her standard company grey suit was cut to fit her rounded bosom, tapering a little at the waist. Her smooth skin was the color of the golden brown crystal Cat had admired back at his apartment. Maybe being dragged here for questioning wasn't such a bad thing after all.

"Looks like he left you here to guard me," he said. "Sure you can handle it?"

"Do you think I can't?"

Ah, this was going to be good. "I'm not sure what you can handle. But I'd like to find out."

She blinked a few times, her mouth partly open. Good. He'd thrown her off a bit.

"What did you say?"

"When is he coming back?" Jon pointed towards the door. "I'd rather talk to the Leader and not one of his little helpers."

He knew he'd hit a nerve when she uncrossed her arms and came to her feet. They were practically eye-to-eye, which surprised him. Other than his mother, he hadn't met many women close to his height.

"It would be better if you stopped talking," she said.

Of course it would, but he had no plans to do that. "What will you do if I don't?" He liked seeing the flash in her brown eyes. Especially the way the golden flecks shimmered against the brown.

Nadira took a step towards him just as the door opened again. Brant strode back into the office and addressed Jonathan.

"You can go now," he said.

Finally he could get out of here. With a nod to Nadira, Jon left the room.

Out in the corridor Matt was talking to a short woman in a dark brown suit. When she saw Jon, she abruptly turned and scooted down the corridor.

"Matt!" Jonathan was glad to see him. "How did you know where I was?"

"One of my company contacts told me you were picked up." He pressed his palm against the lift sensor plate. "Someone is going to answer for hauling you in here."

"I used my father's account to get the shuttle passes, so what?" The lift doors opened and Jon followed him inside.

"So what?" Matt waited for the doors to close before he continued. "They're strict here when it comes to stealing. That's the worst offence you could be charged with."

Jonathan sighed and leaned against the metal paneled wall. "It's my father's account and his security clearance. What the hell was I stealing? They had Guardians question me over shuttle tickets?"

"Guardians questioned you?" Matt grimaced. "We'll talk more when we get to my place."

"Why did you let him go?" Nadira asked. Jonathan Keel used his father's security clearance fraudulently. He should've been sent back to his planet and barred from returning to Hathor.

"One of the company executives ordered us to release him." Brant was staring out the window, his hands clasped behind him. His usual pose when he was deep in thought. "You read him. Was he involved?"

"No. He was deceived by Ilana Travac." Using her abilities to read Jonathan had been very easy. His emotions were close to the surface, as was his arrogance.

But she'd detected something about him that was unexpected. It reminded her of a time when she'd tried unsuccessfully to read another Guardian. A rebound of energy had hit her, making her head ache for hours afterwards. Jonathan's energy had also rebounded, which was unusual for someone without abilities.

And the way he was looking at her--how dare he? Instead of giving her the respect she was due as a Guardian, he'd behaved like a spoiled company brat.

Tall and muscular, he looked more like someone suited to physical labor than the pampered son of a company executive. On Hathor, members of the executive class shunned manual work. Maybe things were different on Jon's home planet, Astarte.

His dark, curly hair was cut shorter than the longer styles most company men favored. And when she'd been close to him, her eyes had been drawn to the hint of stubble on his squared face. For the perfection-obsessed, clean-shaven was the norm, the better to show off the results of various chemical and surgical procedures. But what they had to create, Jonathan came by naturally. And he certainly knew it.

The Leader strolled back to his desk and touched the tabletop. More stats scrolled across the opaqued window. "A company records search confirmed that Ilana Travac has a Novacorp ID chip implanted."

"She works for Novacorp?" Company workers, other than Guardians, executives and miners, had ID chips implanted in their forearms. If only Brandon Keel had one, he probably would've been discovered by now.

"No. It must have been done fraudulently."

"She couldn't have stolen Ansi's identity and uploaded it to her own ID chip without a Novacorp security clearance," Nadira said. "Only certain managers have access to those records."

"Correct. Ilana Travac has been assisted by someone in the company." Brant cleared the display. "Unfortunately her ID chip is no longer functioning, or we'd be able to track her."

"Is she marked?" Nadira asked, referring to the tats thieves were given after their first offense. Placed on the side of the face by the ear, they could not be removed. But they could be hidden.

"No," Brant replied. "She's never been apprehended for stealing. Not yet."

"Brandon Keel is still missing," Nadira said. "He has clearance. He might've helped her."

"That is true. He may make contact with his son." Brant folded his arms across his broad chest. "But Novacorp will not detain the CEO of a profitable mine on suspicion alone. His guilt must be proven first."

"Who ordered Jonathan Keel's release? Why not question them?"

The Sentry Leader unfolded his arms and stared at her as though he'd been struck. "No company executives are to be questioned ever. We have no authority over their decisions."

Why did he always defer to the executives at every opportunity? Didn't the Guardians have any authority? Nadira couldn't stop the tired sigh that escaped her lips.

Brant raised a bushy eyebrow at her response. "Track Jonathan Keel's movements. He may lead you to Ilana Travac or to his father. But do not let him know you are following him. We must be discrete when dealing with people at that level."

"But she doesn't need Keel anymore. Why would they hook up?" The last thing Nadira wanted to do was deal with him again.

"Ilana Travac is a suspected thief and killer." The Leader propped himself on the edge of his desk. "She's a dangerous woman who is smart enough not to get caught. If he meets her again, I have no doubt he will need your protection.

6 DECEPTIONS

After she left the Novacorp Administration building, Nadira went straight to the City Park, an area that stretched for several kilometers in the heart of the city. It was her refuge when she wanted to escape from the glass and metal towers that filled the Nova City landscape.

She often spent hours walking through the gardens. Or strolling along the waterfront where the ferry boats regularly transported people to the seaside towns of the North.

Sitting on a wooden bench, staring out over the lush green grass-covered knoll, she hadn't expected to see her Guardian mentor, Zina. In fact, she'd been able to

approach without Nadira detecting her presence be-
forehand.

In keeping with her disciplined manner, Zina's fitted, brown jacket was closed almost to the neck. She
kept her long black hair clipped back, where it hung
down past her shoulders.

An empath by nature, she was skilled at zeroing in
on the vulnerabilities of her targets, allowing her to use
their own energy against them. Zina never wore jewelry or engaged in affectation, other than her expensive
residence and its furnishings.

Without uttering a word of greeting, her mentor sat
on the edge of the bench, her back rigid. She reminded
Nadira of a very tightly coiled spring.

Tell me what happened at the meeting," Zina said,
her almost-black eyes focused like lasers.

Nadira slid closer to the end of the bench, putting
more space between them. Close contact could, at
times, create physical discomfort between Guardians, a
fact that Nadira had learned early in her training.

"Jonathan Keel was brought in for questioning. But
an exec wanted him released. I don't understand why
Brant let him go on the orders of a company bureaucrat."

"The Sentry Leader is also a bureaucrat. He's not a
real Sentry and he certainly isn't leading anything,"
Zina said, a slight smile on her lips.

Nadira had always been suspicions of Brant. But this was the first time Zina had revealed this information. "Then why is he in that position?"

"Someone has to appear to be in control. And it's in our interests to let the company think they are. But you will find out why in time." She whisked away a leaf that had drifted down from one of the trees. "Did anyone else come with Jonathan Keel?"

"Yes, a woman named is Ilana Travac."

At the mention of Travac's name, Zina's head whisked towards Nadira like it had been jerked. "She wasn't brought in?"

"She and Keel were separated at the terminal."

"Can you track her?"

"Brant told me to track Jonathan Keel."

Zina slapped her hand down on the bench. "He's a fool. If we allow the thieves to elude us, it will reveal to the company that the Guardians are vulnerable. That must never happen."

She'd heard these words often enough over the years. Any failure could be interpreted as weakness, and that could lead Novacorp to question why Guardians were needed at all.

"There's something else," Nadira continued. "Travac doesn't work for Novacorp, but she has a company ID chip implanted. And she's a suspect in the death of a mining operations director named Cintra Ansi."

Zina clasped her hands in her lap. "She must be involved in the robbery on Demeter. We must locate her."

Though Nadira usually couldn't read the emotions of other Guardians, Zina's growing displeasure was hard for her to ignore.

"We can look at connections between her and Novacorp management. Find out how she got the ID chip," Nadira offered.

Zina shook her head. "If her contact in the company was still helping her, she wouldn't have needed to use Jonathan Keel to get here."

"Then should I continue to track him?" Nadira could almost feel sorry for him for being deceived by Travac, but she didn't want to.

"Yes. She'll dispose of him now that he's no longer necessary. That is how she works. He can be our bait to catch her."

Walking into Matt's apartment, Jon was drawn to the floor-to-ceiling windows that lined the entire space. Dropping his bag on a nearby chair, he strolled over to take in the Nova City skyline, where silver, gold and jewel-tone spires glistened against the darkening sky.

"Overwhelming, isn't it?" Matt was at his bar pouring himself a drink. "Want one?" He held out the crystal liquor decanter.

"Not right now," Jonathan replied. "There's nothing like this view on Astarte. How long have you had this place?"

"Got it after I opened my club." Matt led them over to the seating area opposite the window. "Tell me what happened with the Guardians."

"I used my father's security clearance to get our passes for the shuttle. Then I used his account to reserve the room at the Emerald Club. Mine security locked his account this morning."

Matt sighed. "Your father is missing and under suspicion. Are you surprised they alerted security?"

"When you put it that way, no."

"Wait a minute--you said, 'our?'"

Should he tell Matt everything? Could he trust him? Did he have a choice? "A woman came with me. She overheard the thieves on the shuttle. They found out and threatened her."

"What the hell? Where is she?"

Good question. Now if only he had an answer. "I don't know. She's the one I was chasing at the terminal."

"Why did you bring her here? She should've talked to security at the mine," Matt said.

Jonathan shook his head. "She was afraid. She needed my help. I came with her to make sure she'd be all right." Sitting here telling Matt about it now, he realized how ridiculous it sounded. He should've convinced her to talk to Cat.

Matt sipped his drink. "Who is she?"

"I met her about a month ago when she came to my club." Jonathan stared out at the city scene in front of him. "Her name is Ilana Travac. The Guardians think she's a criminal."

"Ilana?" Matt slammed his glass down on the table in front of them and jumped up from the couch. "Damn it, Jonathan! Why didn't you tell me about this?" Matt looked like he was about to punch a hole in the wall.

"What's wrong? Do you know her?"

Matt held out a hand to silence him. "Wait here." He stormed out of the living area, his footsteps pounding against the stone floor.

In another part of the apartment, a door slammed hard enough to rattle the glasses on the bar shelves. What was going on? Whatever was happening, he had no intention of waiting. Instead, Jonathan went after him. At the end of the corridor, stood an imposing set of gold metallic double doors.

Tempted to lean against them to hear what was happening on the other side, he stopped. If he went too close, he might trip the sensor and they'd open. But as it turned out Matt's voice was loud enough to be heard very clearly.

"You don't understand. We have a problem here," Matt bellowed.

Was someone in the room with him? No, he was probably using a com unit. But who was he talking to?

"Yes, he brought her here! You should've stopped it."

Straining to listen, he moved closer, his fingers slight millimeters away from the shiny metal door. When Matt spoke again, his voice was so low that it could barely be heard.

"I know, I know. I'll take care of it. He's going to have to go..."

Jon backed away from the door. He'd trusted Matt and that had been a mistake.

Heading back out to the living area, Jonathan shot a glance over his shoulder. Matt was his father's friend, but if he tried anything, Jon would have to defend himself.

There was no point in staying here any longer. He grabbed his travel bag and left the apartment. If he wanted to find out what happened to his father, he'd have to do it on his own.

7 Pursuit

Nadira lingered in the park after her meeting with Zina. Her next step was to track Jonathan Keel. Would he want her help? Most likely not. He thought he was smarter than everyone else. But it didn't matter. Keel was on her planet now and her territory.

Drawing in a deep breath, she closed her eyes and focused, waiting for the pictures to form in her mind. She saw Keel riding in a transport with an older man. Both men exited the vehicle and walked into a building.

There was a name over the entrance in silver letters. What was it? The scene was fading. Wait--what was the name...she could still make out some of the letters...D...I...A...M...O...N...of course. It had to be the

Diamond Star apartment tower. Keel was at one of the most expensive residences in the Palatine.

Fifteen minutes later Nadira was standing across the boulevard from the tower.

Transport traffic was becoming congested, as was the foot traffic along the marbled sidewalks. In front of her, passengers queued up for transport vehicles. Company workers in their somber suits jockeyed for position with festively attired tourists.

Nova City's ground transport system covered the entire megalopolis. For pedestrians, wide sidewalks, automated people movers and footbridges traversed the various districts, easing the congestion of the traffic lanes.

Standing out of the way so she wouldn't get jostled, Nadira scanned the tower. Each floor had tinted glass walls that kept her from seeing what was going on inside. Was Keel looking down at her right now from one of the apartments?

On Hathor being the son of a CEO was nothing special. The planet was filled with them. Nadira smiled to herself. Keel thought he was untouchable because of his father's connections. Yet his emotions were so easy to read. Dealing with him wasn't a challenge at all. If only he'd come out of that building right now. Seeing her there would wipe that arrogant smirk off his face.

Jonathan watched the floor numbers tick off as he rode down in the lift. The entire front was clear glass, giving him a view of the marbled lobby as he descended. People were moving around below. But he didn't detect anyone dressed in security garb.

The lift stopped and the door swept aside, allowing him a quick exit. Before he reached the entrance, a holographic attendant appeared, asking if he needed transportation.

Maybe that was a good idea. He could get back to the Emerald Club. And if Ilana showed up, even better. It was time to get some truth from her too.

Yes, I need a transport," he said.

Dressed in a form-fitting gold dress that matched the lobby interior, the holo motioned towards the doorway. "Please step outside and your vehicle will arrive shortly," she instructed, before her image disappeared.

Jonathan looked up at the floor he'd come from. The half-walls that ringed each level were clear enough to give him a view if Matt were following him. No, there was no one up there.

When he stepped outside, transport vehicles were crowding the traffic lanes as aircars whizzed overhead. He heard strains of music off in the distance. Maybe once he checked in at the Emerald Club, he'd head back out and see what the entertainments were like.

Down at the curb, a sparkling white vehicle pulled over and stopped in front of him. Across the street people were lined up waiting for transports. From the looks of them, they were Novacorp workers. Why did they all dress in those boring suits? Even miners' overalls had more color.

Standing back to let the transport door slide open, he scanned the area. No security in sight. Good. They were leaving him alone. Jon was about to climb into the vehicle when he saw a familiar face across the street. Wasn't that Nadira, the Guardian? No. He had to be mistaken.

Wait. A few pedestrians filed past her, blocking his view for a moment. She was looking up at the tower. Squinting as though she could see inside it. What was she looking for?

Their eyes met. Did she just jump, or was he imagining it? Oh no. She did react. He was sure of it. What the hell did she think she was doing by following him? He looked at the transport, then back over at Nadira. Was that a smirk on her face? Damn it. She was daring him to come over there.

So, she thought she could just track him across the city and he couldn't do anything about it? It didn't matter to him if she was a Guardian, or whatever she called herself. He wasn't going to be treated like a common thief.

Jonathan hitched up the strap of his travel bag. He wouldn't even bother to use the pedestrian bridge. It was half a block away and would take too much time.

Walking around the transport, he stepped into the street. There was a break in the traffic. If he moved fast, he could make it across without a problem. The transports were programmed to stop for obstructions. But whether they could stop short if he ran out in front of them was another matter.

Nadira darted down the side street. She wouldn't get far. Jonathan dodged a couple of passing vehicles on his way across the boulevard.

He made it to the opposite corner and in his haste, banged into a company worker. Flashing Jonathan a scowl, the man smoothed his dark brown jacket. But Jon didn't have time to apologize. Nadira was up ahead, just a beat away from running.

Not that it mattered if she ran. He knew he could get her. She was obviously fit. But he had longer legs. And a lot of practice catching what he wanted.

"Nadira!" He called out, reminding her that he was still there.

Ignoring him, she kept up the pace. Skillfully weaving between the oncoming pedestrians without touching them. She moved gracefully. He enjoyed watching her. Just like he was enjoying the chase. But unless she could disappear like a holo, she wasn't going to escape him.

She was at the corner now. There was a footbridge arched over the street. He could make out throngs of people streaming across. Lights on the other side of the bridge illuminated the sky. And he could hear music.

Must be an entertainment area. If she went across the bridge, she'd get jammed up in the crowd.

She dashed up the ramp. Now he knew he had her. He slowed his pace as he approached the bridge. A small group of tourists exited as he got on the ramp. Two of the women were laughing, their faces animated as they clung to each other. What a contrast to the woman he was pursuing. Nadira acted like she'd rather be locked in a mineshaft than to show any humor.

Jon strode across the bridge. Could she sense him coming? He hoped so. By now she had to know she wasn't going to get away from him.

When she got down the ramp, Nadira stood off to the side, waiting. She wasn't smirking anymore. But she wasn't fearful either. Instead, she glared at him, her brown eyes defiant, her lips pursed. Funny, the more annoyed she tried to be, the more amused and attracted he was.

"So, we meet again," he said. "Why did you run away?"

"I wasn't running."

"Okay, you weren't. Why were you watching me? I thought I was cleared."

She looked away for a moment, composing her thoughts. "You're not under suspicion, Mr. Keel. But Ilana Travac is."

"Then why follow me? I told you I don't know where she is."

"She might contact you."

"Why can't you find her? Don't you have special Guardian powers or something?"

She stiffened. So, Nadira didn't like to be questioned. Good. He didn't like being questioned either.

"I don't have 'special Guardian powers.' I have abilities that allow me to read people's emotions and to--"

Jon waved her away. "Okay, no need to explain it all. By the way, have you had dinner?"

Her mouth hung open for a few seconds before she responded. "What did you say?"

"Dinner. I haven't eaten since I got off the shuttle. Is there somewhere to go around here?" He motioned towards the shops and restaurants that lined plaza. "Lots of places to choose from."

"I--I--yes, I eat dinner," she said. "But I'm not supposed to--"

"Eat dinner with someone you're following? Why not? You want information? I'll tell you what I know. Then you'll tell me what I want to know. How about that?" He smiled, hoping it would affect her the way it did most women he encountered.

"All right."

"Lead the way." He felt strangely exhilarated. Standing here close to her, his body was reacting in ways he didn't want to think about right now. There was something beneath the surface that intrigued him. He had to find out more about her.

8 WELCOME TO HATHOR

After dinner they walked through the plaza, which was still bustling and showed no signs of quieting down. Overhead, the moons, Isis and Osiris resembled two golden orbs in the night sky. Though with all the floodlights illuminating the square, to Nadira it looked more like midday than evening.

She was surprised that their conversation during dinner had gone so well. Jon told her that Matt Bento, who had picked him up from the Administration building, was one of Brandon Keel's oldest friends.

As soon as she'd heard the name, she knew why he lived in a place like the Diamond Star. Bento was a prominent and wealthy businessman and had recently opened a private club for Novacorp executives.

Throughout their meal Jonathan had been very charming. She'd sat across from him in a private lounge of a very expensive restaurant. She'd never had enough credits to eat there, but Jonathan's supply seemed inexhaustible. He'd even persuaded her to try some seafood delicacies from the North Country, the area where she and mother had lived.

"You don't eat much, do you?" Jonathan asked.

"I wasn't as hungry as you were, obviously."

"When security picked me up, they didn't ask if I'd had lunch." He chuckled. "Still can't believe I actually ate real chicken. It's sort of funny that when the first settlers came here from Earth they brought chicken with them. You'd think they would've thought of something better."

"The First Families wanted to bring things from Earth that would survive and remind them of home."

"First Families? What's that?"

"The seven families who were selected from the different lands on Earth. They were the first people to settle here. The Guardians are descended from them."

"Are you serious? How could just seven families populate a planet this size?" Jonathan scoffed. "Who told you that?"

Of course he would act superior. What did he know about Hathor or its people? "It's a story that was passed down to remind us of where we came from. I didn't say that other people didn't settle here as well.

It's supposed to be symbolic. Didn't anyone in your family ever tell you stories?"

"Sure, my mot--I mean, my father never had time for stories. He was busy with the mine," Jonathan replied.

She was certain that Jonathan was holding something back from her. What was he hiding? As much as she was able to read him, there was a part of him that was locked down. It felt like a wall that was impossible to break through. He had to be hiding something very important. Maybe it was about Ilana Travac's whereabouts--or his father's.

"Mr. Keel, are you certain no one has been in contact with you since you arrived?"

"You asked that question already at dinner, and I answered: no. And, it's 'Jonathan.' Remember?" He hitched his travel bag across his body.

"I remember."

When they got to the footbridge, it was still clogged with pedestrians streaming back and forth. Straining to keep as much space as possible between herself and the people around her, she folded her arms across her chest as she walked.

Even the slightest contact could leave her reeling from the emotions of the person she touched. Normally Nadira was able to relax and let the feelings pass through her. But right now, surrounded by so many people, she felt a bit overwhelmed.

At the base of the footbridge, she noticed that Jon was staring at her. Better not to let him see how uncomfortable she was. She dropped her arms to her sides.

"Where to now?" Jon asked, as he watched the transports moving past.

"You never mentioned why you decided not to stay with Matt Bento."

"We had a difference of opinion."

He wasn't going to share anything more right now. In fact, she could feel the tension underneath his calm expression. "Are you going back home?"

Jonathan glared at her. "I'm not going anywhere until I find out what happened to my father. Besides, the shuttle for Astarte doesn't leave for 5 days. I couldn't go now if I wanted to."

A couple walked past them, so wrapped up in each other that they bumped into Jonathan. He absently nodded to them as they apologized, then continued on.

"Guess we're in the way," he said, as he took her arm and led her over to the side. "Look, I'm going to the Emerald Club to check in. Why don't you come with me?"

Why was he standing so close? Did he realize how hard it was to look into those grey eyes and stay focused on her work? Not to mention she wasn't used to having to look up to make eye contact with anyone.

Jon was very much aware of the effect he had on women. All that smiling and touching. He knew ex-

actly what he was doing to her. But she was determined to keep her distance and stay detached. No
matter how hard she had to work at it.

She placed her hands against his chest and nudged
him. He took a step back, but she felt him resist being
moved more than that. Underneath her palms she
could feel his heartbeat pulsing against her. It was
causing all kinds of reactions in her body that she did-
n't want to think about right now.

"Do you like touching me?" he asked, a slow smile
on his lips.

She jerked her hands away as though she'd been
burned. "You don't have to stand so close."

"I thought we were friends. We just had dinner did-
n't we? Come walk with me. We can talk on the way."

She didn't want to go anywhere with him. How
dare he ask her such a thing. Who did he think he
was?

"I could use your help. Okay?"

Another smile. Why did he keep doing that? Brant
had instructed her to protect Jon. And who knows,
Ilana Travac might show up. Yes, it made sense to go
with him. It was part of her job.

"We should take a transport," Nadira replied. "It'll
be quicker."

Inside the vehicle, Jonathan stretched out his legs
on the opposite seat. The cushions were rather com-

fortable. And as the vehicle trundled along the streets, he had to fight to keep his eyes open.

"Nova Entertainments welcomes you!"

Startled, he jumped up. "What? Who said that?"

"It's from up there. We're coming into the Entertainment district," Nadira replied.

Through the clear roof of the transport he saw a huge vid screen projecting images of people dancing, laughing, and walking. Aircars zoomed by, swooping down to avoid other craft.

Music blasted from the clubs and restaurants, one tune mixing with another and another until he couldn't tell where one ended and the next began. The bustle on the streets was waking him up. Jon patted the seat cushion to the beat.

"Do you come to this district often?" he asked, guessing what her answer would be.

"I have no reason to."

Based on Nadira's discomfort when they were in the plaza, he could tell she didn't like crowds. Even sitting here in the transport she'd left as much space between them as possible. If she moved over any more, she'd be outside.

"You don't like having fun? he asked.

"Not when I'm working, Mr. Keel."

"It's Jonathan. Remember? Say it with me: Jonathan."

She gave him a withering look. "Jonathan."

"Much better." That wasn't so hard. Just give him enough time. He'd get her to loosen up.

Nadira got out of the transport first. She'd heard a lot about the Emerald club. It was one of the most expensive hotels in the city. But this was the first time she'd seen it up close.

Her attention was drawn to two male security officers to the right of the entrance. They were in a heated discussion, their gestures animated. Dressed in black uniforms, they looked like city security. But they weren't wearing the standard helmets. They were probably private guards for the hotel.

Nadira joined Jonathan as he climbed out of the vehicle. "Are you sure this is a good idea? Matt knows where you were going to stay. If he wants to find you--"

"I don't know what he's into, but I'll be careful." He slung his bag over his shoulder. "Why don't you come up with me?"

"I have to go now." She didn't want to go inside. And she certainly wasn't going upstairs with him either.

He brushed his fingers along her arm. "Look, we can help each other, just like we talked about at dinner. There's no record of my father coming here. So if we find Ilana, we can make her tell us what happened at the mine. We can do it together."

"I didn't say we were going to look for her together." Nadira stepped back. Why was it he was always standing so close? "If she contacts you, let me know right away. Don't do anything on your own."

He smiled. "Come in with me. Maybe she's waiting inside."

"That's highly unlikely, Jonathan. But let's see if she left a message for you."

He flashed her a charming smile, his grey eyes warm and very inviting. Inviting her to what? She wasn't sure she wanted to know.

As soon as they walked into the lobby, the attendant greeted them with a smile. "Mr. Keel! You've returned. Is this your guest? Was everything taken care of with your father's account?"

"This is a friend of mine, Mr. Renard. I'll use my account instead," Jonathan replied.

Nadira felt energy pings shoot through her as Jon touched her arm to guide her. Flinching, she steadied herself as she sat next to him.

"Any messages left for me?" Jon asked.

"There were no messages," Renard said. "If you would place your palm on the sensor plate, we'll use your ID to access your credits."

Nadira drew in a deep breath. Her heart rate was speeding up, alerting her to something on the edge of her consciousness. But what was it? Once she got away from Jonathan it would help. It was getting harder to keep her emotions from being affected by his.

When the attendant was finished getting Jon's information, he directed them to the lift. Next to it, the smiling face of a computer-generated woman appeared.

"Good evening, Mr. Keel," she said in a low, raspy voice. "My name is Lorena. Will you be staying long?"

"Just a few days," he replied.

"Jonathan, I have to leave now." Nadira wanted to put some distance between them. "I'll contact you tomorrow."

He reached out to touch her. But she moved away before he could make contact.

"Are you sure? Why don't you come up for a bit?"

"I have to go. We'll talk tomorrow."

Not wanting to wait for his reply, she hurried away. Behind her she heard the "swoosh" of the lift doors closing. She could still feel his emotions though, and she was unable to block his feelings of disappointment at her sudden departure.

Outside in the fresh air her heartbeat slowed, allowing her to relax and focus again. The transport was still waiting at the curb. But as she was about to take a step, she stopped.

Out of the corner of her eye she detected movement. The two security officers had stopped talking and were rushing towards the entrance. Nadira's body tingled as she watched them.

There was a threat nearby. But who was in danger?

The guards entered the building. She ran over to where they'd been standing. Closing her eyes, she concentrated on the energy trail they'd left behind.

Pictures began to form in her mind along with snippets of their conversation. They'd argued over instructions they'd been given...over orders to bring someone from this hotel to another location...and if the person didn't come willingly...they were to do whatever was necessary.

"May I help you?"

Behind her, the smiling face of a holo was displayed on the glass wall of the building.

"Do you require assistance? Would you like a transport?" he asked, breaking into a broad smile. His greenish gold hair matched the shimmering surface. Unfortunately his bright green eyes were a bit disconcerting.

"No, I don't need one, thank you."

"Would you like to know about the opening of the new entertainment complex?"

Was there a way to stop him from talking? Another picture materialized in her mind. The guards were at a door...there was a sign next to it that read, "Alpha." Now the door was slowly opening and--

"May I recommend a new café nearby? It has been given the highest approval rating by Novacorp Entertainments."

"I'm not hungry!" she shouted.

"Are you certain you do not require a transport?" He was still smiling, his green eyes glowing as he worked to please her.

She closed her eyes and saw the guards again...the door was open and they were pushing their way inside...Jonathan was visible for a few seconds...then the door closed.

Nadira ran back inside. "Where is Jonathan Keel staying?" She held up her left hand, identifying herself as a Guardian.

Mr. Renard's eyes grew wide. "A Guardian! What has happened?"

"Where is he?"

"He's--he's on level 30 suite Alpha." Renard replied, his voice shaking so much he barely got the words out. "Is he in danger? At the Emerald Club we ensure the safety of all our guests and--"

"Call city security now!" Nadira yelled, rushing to the lift.

Inside, Lorena's image appeared on the wall next to the door. "Welcome to the Emerald Club. Where would you like to go?"

"Level 30 right away!"

The doors closed and the lift headed up. It was so quiet that for a moment Nadira wasn't sure it was moving. But a moment later she heard a soft female voice in the background.

"3...4...5...6..."

Lorena was still smiling. At least she didn't have bright green eyes like the man downstairs. Lorena's were a subdued golden brown.

"You'll find the city has a great deal of entertainment. Would you like to know more?" Lorena asked.

"12...13...14...15"

"Not right now." Nadira closed eyes. Nothing materialized. Why couldn't she see what was happening in the suite? She paced as each level ticked by. Why was the lift moving so slowly?

"20...21...22...23"

"Can't this go any faster?" she asked.

"I'm sorry. The safety of our guests is most important to us, and we can't--"

"Okay, Lorena. I get it."

"27...28...29..."

At level 30 Nadira jumped out as soon as the door opened. In front of her, a sign indicated that suite Alpha was to her left. She broke into a run, her feet pounding the stone floor. A gold-toned door stood at the end of the corridor.

She touched the fingerpad. Nothing. It must be locked. More noises from inside: the hum of a weapon discharge and glass shattering.

By now her heart was slamming in her chest. Pings of energy flooded her body. She had to get in there now. Summoning all her strength, Nadira pressed her palms against the door and directed her force into it.

Within seconds the door went from gold to bright white, then blue. Her energy burned through it. White-hot sparks flew up, pinging against the walls as the door disintegrated, then blew apart.

Almost pushed off her feet by the force of the blast, Nadira caught herself before she fell. Inside the suite, one guard was on his knees, the other had an arm around Jon's neck. They'd stopped in mid-action, staring at her through the smoldering remains.

Jonathan recovered quickly and got out from under his attacker. He took the man's arm and twisted it behind him. Still on his knees, the other guard glared at her as he reached for his weapon. He staggered to his feet and aimed it at her.

As he raised his hand, Jon released the man he'd been struggling with. He launched himself forward and knocked the guard to the ground. He and the armed man struggled, each fighting for control. The weapon discharged. A bright golden blast of heat burned into the couch.

Nadira turned her attention to the guard that Jon had pushed away. The man reached under his uniform jacket. She directed a blast of energy towards him. Clutching his chest, he screamed, then fell to his knees.

Careful to shield herself from the energy rebound, she sent out another blast. He fell down on the floor, still trembling. Then he groaned and passed out, his mouth open.

Another weapon discharge filled the air with sparks, the whine setting her teeth on edge. Jonathan fell to the floor. A large, dark patch on his sleeve was hissing and smoking. The guard stood over him, pointing his weapon at Jon's chest.

Nadira flung a short blast of energy towards the attacker. He screamed, his arms out flung. His weapon flew up in the air and crashed through a glass table across the room. In her haste she hadn't shielded herself and the rebound of the guard's energy hit her like a punch in the stomach. Breathless, she fell to her knees.

The man landed across Jonathan's legs in a heap. She crawled over and pushed at him with her fingertips. In reaction, he moaned before he rolled over on his side and vomited. Nadira struggled to pull Jonathan away from him.

She dropped down and pulled Jon across her lap. His breath was shallow and ragged, his eyes unfocused. The hole in his sleeve was still smoking and she could smell burning flesh.

Gritting her teeth, she pulled back his jacket and lifted up his shirt. The blast had seared a circle of skin below his left shoulder, leaving it burned and oozing.

Jonathan opened his eyes wide, studying her face. Then without a word he went limp, his head rolling over to the side.

"Jonathan!" She cradled his body, burying her face against him. Let him be all right.

She'd been charged with protecting him. And she'd failed.

9 TAKEN IN

Hours later Nadira was sprawled across her couch. Her clothes were in a crumpled heap on the floor. After arriving, she'd been too tired to put them away properly.

Replaying the events at the hotel in her mind, she still couldn't believe she was capable of such destruction. The knowledge was both exciting and frightening. Through all of her development and training with Zina, the depth of her abilities had never been revealed.

Nadira heard a noise from her bedroom. Sitting up was agony. Lifting herself up on rubbery legs, she waited for the room to stop spinning. It could be hours or days before she regained her full strength. Until then, it was all she could do to put one foot in front of the other.

Jonathan was in her bed, the covers up to his waist. The medi-evac team had managed to apply regenerating skin to the burns on his arm and chest. Other than the itching he'd have to endure while the new skin grafted onto his own, he was going to be fine. His clothes were the only real casualty. What hadn't been torn in the struggle had been ripped away by the medics.

"What...what happened? He swallowed. "I feel like I've been hit by a transport."

Nadira sat on the edge of the bed. "You were hit with a blast from a stunner. It uses energy to incapacitate, like using an electrical current. They use larger versions in the mines."

Struggling to sit up, he shifted himself against the pillows. "They're used for mining Crysallis."

"You've been inside the mines?"

He nodded. "With my father."

Jon slowly lifted the covers and examined himself. "Where are my clothes?" he asked.

"The medics removed them. Don't worry, you were covered when they brought you here."

"Where's 'here?'"

Nadira paused a moment before answering. Mr. Renard at the Emerald Club had suggested taking him to another suite. She hadn't trusted it. Instead she had the medics bring him to a place where no one would be looking for him.

"You're at my apartment. I thought it would be safer," she replied.

Were those men real security guards?" he asked.

"I doubt it. They've been taken to detention to be questioned. Don't think about it right now. I'll let you get back to sleep."

"Nadira?"

"Yes?"

"Don't leave yet," he whispered, reaching out to her.

As a Guardian she was always supposed to stay detached. But following procedure had never been her strong suit--something else she'd inherited from her mother, Minona.

Nadira sighed and clasped his hand, letting his fingers intertwine with her own. She felt a gentle tug and she eased herself down next to him.

"You can get under the covers you know."

"This is fine. Get some rest."

She remained there and watched him as he fell asleep. Not long after, she gave in to exhaustion and drifted off.

When Jonathan woke up the room was dark. For a moment he thought he was back home in his own bed. No, this wasn't his bedroom. He was on Hathor. Now he remembered. He'd been hit by a stunner blast. And Nadira had brought him here.

During the fight he'd held up his arm to shield himself from the blast. Running his hand over the wound he felt--what the hell? A strip of rough, knitted fabric was attached to his skin. How did this get on him? Whatever the thing was, he had to get it off. Ah, there it was. He caught an edge of the fabric between his thumb and index finger and pulled.

"Damn!" he roared.

"Lights up 70%," Nadira called out.

"What is this thing? It hurts like hell."

"It's regenerating skin. Stop picking at it."

He held out his arm for her inspection, wincing as she examined the graft.

"The medics said it'll be completely attached in a couple of days. What about your chest?"

"My chest?"

Nadira leaned across him. With a light touch she probed the small, yellow patch below his collarbone. Though he couldn't feel anything through the fake skin, the proximity of her body next to his was enough to take his mind off the pain.

She was wearing a tank top. Her full, golden brown breasts were straining against the creamy knitted fabric, presenting him with a very tantalizing view of her cleavage.

"So, how does it look?" Unable to resist, he glided his hands over her back. Keeping his gaze fixed on her, he lifted himself up, opening his lips in anticipation of meeting hers and--

"That's enough of that, Mr. Keel." With a wry smile, she eased herself out of his grasp and scooted back to the other side of the bed.

"Trust me, there can never be enough of that." He sat up and ran his fingers through his hair. "I'd better get cleaned up."

"Let me get you something to put on."

Nadira eased off the bed and padded over to a set of shelves in a corner of the room. There was little more than a strip of lace covering her bottom, which was just fine because it gave him a very delicious view of her firm hips.

Searching through the rows of neatly folded clothing, she pulled out a light grey shirt.

"That won't fit me," he said.

"I know. It's for me." She smiled as she slipped it on and secured the front.

Damn. She was the most exasperating woman he'd ever met.

Returning with pants and a t-shirt, she held them out. "I know this isn't what you're used to. You can wear these until we get your things from the hotel," she said.

A quick glance at them and he could tell they were the same grey, knitted underalls that miners wore under their work gear. Stretchy enough to fit a variety of body types, they could also be scratchy as hell.

"Thanks." He pulled back the covers and swung his legs out. Stretching, he came to his feet. The stone floor was cold. Maybe his boots were around here someplace.

"I'll give you some privacy." Nadira took a step back and banged against the wall, missing the doorway by several centimeters

"It's not like we're strangers," he said, amused at her efforts to keep eye contact with him. "Besides, you saw everything when they brought me in last night. Didn't you?"

Her eyes darted to a lower part of his anatomy, then back up again. "I wasn't looking."

"I'm sure you were." He grinned as he grabbed the pants and shook them out.

Rolling her eyes, she left the room. A moment later he heard footsteps, followed by a crash.

"Are you all right?" he asked.

"I forgot I left my clothes on the floor. I'm fine!" she snapped.

Chuckling to himself, he pulled on the pants and cinched the drawstring. Did these belong to a regular companion of hers, or someone she was contracted with? Did Guardians go into contracted relationships?

Based on the lack of personal effects in her bedroom, he didn't see any evidence of a partner. Other than the bed, table and built-in shelves, there wasn't much else in the room. It looked barely lived in.

When he entered the living area, the sun was shining brightly through a row of large windows. From the looks of things outside, they were in a residential district. Across the street was a large stone building with windows like Nadira's. Transports rumbled by, though there weren't as many as he'd seen on the main boulevards.

The small but comfortable living area opened up into a dining space with a counter and two seats. Nadira was sitting on one of the stools, her legs dangling.

"I don't have a lot on hand for breakfast, so if you want something more, I'll order it," she said.

"No problem."

Though it was neat and clean, the apartment showed signs of wear. Instead of shiny silver, the countertop was dull and scratched. Even the cooker looked like it'd seen better days.

"Shower's over there." She motioned to a half-open pocket door to her right.

He slid the door back and looked inside. It was a long, narrow space lined with grey and white marble walls and a shower enclosure at the end. Next to the shower sat the sink and toilet, crammed next to each other like an afterthought.

Utilitarian design at its best: clean, efficient and exceptionally boring. Maybe this apartment building had originally been designed to house miners. It wasn't the type of place he expected a Guardian to live in.

"Looks cozy. I guess you don't share it with any-one," he said

"No."

"No family?"

Her face stiffened. "Not anymore."

"Oh. Sorry." What was her story? He wanted to ask, but the scowl on her face made him think better of it.

"You can take your shower now," she said.

"Sure you don't want to go first?"

"I'll wait. I have something to do." Stone-faced, she folded her arms across her chest.

"Okay." For some reason she was annoyed with him. No doubt it wouldn't be the last time.

While Jon was in the shower, Nadira picked up her tablet and settled herself on the couch. The attack had to be involved with the theft from the mine. If she could look at the mine security report, it might give her a clue about who sent the men. Nadira tapped the screen with her stylus.

The clear glass displayed her location and the temperature. 25 degrees Celsius was typical this time of year in the climate-controlled environs of Nova City.

After 45 minutes of searching through the Demeter mine records, she couldn't find any mention of the robbery. Instead of a detailed report on the incident, she found endless records about the number of crystals mined, personnel hired and even orders of food and machinery. But not one mention of the theft.

There had to be a mistake. She aborted the search and contacted Brant. He answered her right away, which was unusual since he normally kept her waiting.

"Nadira," he said, his jowly face filling the screen. "I was informed of the incident at the Emerald Club last night. Were you harmed?"

"No, Sentry Leader, I was not. I have a question--"

"An armed attack on a citizen--a CEO's son no less--in the Palatine district is unthinkable. The attackers will be severely punished."

Impatient to ask her question, she interrupted him. "I've been investigating the robbery on Demeter. The security reports about the incident no longer exist. Do you know why?" she asked.

There was silence for a moment. Brant cleared his throat before responding. "Why are you searching? You already know as much as you need to."

As much as she needed to? Was he serious? "It's my responsibility to know. How can I do my job if I don't have all the facts?"

"Have you located Ilana Travac?"

"Where's the report?" she asked, her hands gripping the sides of the tablet. "You haven't answered my question, Sentry Leader."

Brant shifted in his chair. "Those records have been locked, Nadira."

"Guardians have access to all security records, or have you forgotten?" She didn't care if she insulted him. "You have no right to restrict me from seeing that report."

"I have every right. Your only responsibility is to follow orders," he barked.

Nadira gritted her teeth, willing herself not to respond to his dismissive tone. If she gripped her tablet any harder, it might break in two.

"I am a Sentry--a real one." She let that sink in before she continued, "I have a job to do. Give me access to the information."

By now Brant's putty-colored face was flushed with red. His cheeks puffed and his bushy brows were lifted up like two half-moons. She hadn't planned to use the information Zina had given her about his title of "Sentry Leader" being purely honorary. But she'd had about enough of his attitude. Jonathan could've been killed last night. She wasn't in the mood for bureaucratic nonsense.

"How dare you! I am the leader here, not you. I will give the orders!"

"Jonathan Keel was attacked and his father is missing. Don't you think there's a connection?"

Brant opened his mouth as if to reply, then he froze. She heard talking in the background, but couldn't make what was being said.

"Demeter Mine Security Chief Catherine Mantee requested that we refrain from further investigations into the whereabouts of Brandon Keel."

"Why? He's still missing, isn't he?"

"Chief Mantee informed us that remains were found last night in the mine. It has not been confirmed, but CEO Keel should be presumed dead."

Nadira gasped. Jon's father was dead? He was so sure his father left Demeter before the explosion. "If the remains were found last night, why hasn't it been confirmed yet?"

"You were there last night when the officers arrived. But their report does not include what happened to Keel."

"Must be an oversight." As she'd requested, the officers hadn't added Jon's location to their report. But that wasn't a fact she was going to share with Brant.

"There is no record of Jonathan Keel being admitted at the medi-evac. And he is not at his hotel."

"I don't know where he is," she lied. "Why are you looking for him?"

"Brandon Keel had ownership in the mine. If he's dead, his son is his only heir. He must be located as soon as possible so that proper company procedures can be followed." Brant's words tumbled out like he was reciting a script he'd been programmed to say.

"But if he's expected to take up management of the mine, he should return to Astarte. I repeat, why are you looking for him?"

"If you know where he is, you must divulge the information or you will be in violation."

"You didn't answer my question."

She heard more talking in the background. This time she recognized the voice. It was Zina.

"He had a relationship with the criminal, Ilana Travac. And we suspect his father was complicit in the robbery. If you are shielding him from us, you will be in direct violation and we'll bring you before the Elders."

"Travac deceived him. Jonathan had nothing to do with it."

"As I suspected, you have allowed yourself to be taken in by him. Guardians must never become personally involved. You are well aware of the ramifications of such an action. If not, then remember the fate of your mother."

Nadira almost dropped the tablet. Those words didn't come from Brant, they came from Zina. Her mentor had never forgiven Minona for rejecting her duty as a Guardian. And she was using the Sentry Leader to deliver that message.

"If you want him, find him yourself." Nadira disconnected.

There was something more going on, something that went deeper than the robbery. And now Jonathan was at the center of it.

10 ON THE EDGE

"Guardians must never become personally involved."
The Sentry Leader's words continued to ring in Nadira's ears as she drained the last of her tea and slammed the cup on the counter. How dare Brant lecture her on how to do her job. But it surprised her that Zina would put words into his mouth. What did she have to gain from forcing Jonathan to submit to more questioning?

Unfortunately if Zina took charge of it, the session would be closer to an interrogation. When it came to getting the truth from suspects, Zina's skills were unsurpassed. Though the methods she used were questionable. Forcing your way into someone's mind was no different than forcing yourself into their body.

It was only to be done in extreme cases and when Novacorp sanctioned it. But the robbery on Demeter was the first major theft on that satellite. Company executives would authorize any action to insure the thieves were caught--even if it meant using force on a CEO's son.

She grabbed the teapot and poured hot water into her cup. After crushing a handful of leaves between her fingers, she sprinkled them into a small, metal strainer. One of her pleasures was the make tea this way, as she'd seen it done when she was a child in the North. It took more time, but the flavor was worth the work.

Bobbing the silver strainer in the steaming water, she closed her eyes and inhaled the sweet, citrus scent. An image of the seashore came to her mind, and her mother's smile. Her brown eyes glistening, as she beckoned Nadira to come over to the water's edge. Minona's pink and gold dress flowing in the sea breeze, fluttering like the feathery wings of a bird.

Come to the edge, Nadira. Come to the edge...

The bathroom door slid back and Jon sauntered out, followed by a cloud of steam. He secured the towel around his waist as he joined Nadira at the counter. "That smells great."

Unable to take her eyes off of him, she took a deep swallow before answering. "I'll make you a cup."

In the aftermath of the attack, she'd been too drained to do anything but collapse on the couch. But now, with him standing across from her, wearing nothing but a damp towel, it was a different matter.

His body still moist, his dark hair slicked back, and his tanned skin flushed from the hot shower, her awareness of him was overpowering.

"I'm not a tea drinker. Got any coffee?" he asked, poking around in the cabinet over the built-in cooker.

"Might be some instant packs back there somewhere. Are you hungry yet?"

He shut the cabinet and leaned his elbows against the counter so that they were face-to-face. "Not yet. I've been meaning to tell you. What you did last night--never seen anything like that. How did you know about the guards?"

Jon's skin smelled like fresh, clean soap. She watched a droplet of water slowly make its way down his muscular arm and disappear. Focus, damn it.

"They were outside when I was leaving. I knew they were up to something."

"But how did you know?"

"It's hard to explain. A simple way to put it is that I was able to read their emotions."

"Really? How do you do that?"

"It comes to me as pictures or conversations. It depends. If a target is very agitated, they give off a lot of energy and they're easier to read. Or it can happen if they're very passionate and have very strong emotions."

Jonathan grinned. "So, you were able to track me because I'm passionate or because I have strong emotions?"

"Both." She could feel him now. His desire for her was growing, reaching through the barriers she kept putting between them. Flowing under and around them like a rushing river pushing past every obstruction.

Nadira had never encountered someone without Guardian abilities who was strong enough to overcome her emotional shields. And what was more interesting, he seemed to have no idea he was doing it.

"You saved my life. That means I'm yours." He took her hand, rubbing his thumb over her wrist. "What are you going to do with me?"

Could he feel her trembling? She hoped not. That's all she needed right now. If he had any idea how much he was doing to her, he'd be totally impossible. He was so used to women falling over themselves for him. It was going to be hard, but she was determined not to be one of them.

"Do all Guardians have power like yours?" He continued to glide his fingertips over her skin.

Gulping, she willed her body to stop responding. It wasn't working. His touch was deceptively light. But combined with the force of his energy, her nerve endings were lighting up all over her body.

"For the most part, all Guardians can read thoughts and emotions. Some of us have abilities to

touch objects and read the energy that clings to them."
Her voice faltered, shaking as she watched him come
from behind the counter. "All of the descendents of the
First Families have some ability...but for most of them
it's not strong enough to be developed."

Jonathan approached her. Closing in on her as she
sat helpless on the stool, her body aching in anticipation. Instead of touching her again, he braced himself
against the counter, his sinewy arms trapping her with
no escape.

"So, how can people tell the difference between
Guardians and everyone else?"

His voice was a low growl, his energy surrounding
her in a cocoon of heat and the remnants of fresh soap.
In her mind a picture materialized of him in the
shower, water pouring down on him like a summer
rain. Wiping himself down and leaving trails of soap
along his arms...and chest...and...

"We--we have this." Trembling, she held up her left
hand to show him the half-moon shaped line in her
palm.

"Did they put that there?"

"It forms naturally when we've developed our abilities."

Leaning down, he kissed the side of her face, trailing
kisses across her cheek. "So tell me, what other abilities
do you have?" he asked.

"I--I don't know what you mean." She closed her
eyes as his mouth found hers, his tongue insistent. As

his kiss intensified, she fought the urge to touch him and pull him closer. If she let this go on, she'd be lost.

How could she protect him if she let her physical desires get in the way? Brant and Zina were searching for him. Shielding Jon from them would use all the energy she had left.

Keeping them from tracking him would require her to connect with him, and create a protective wall around him. It was the only way to keep them from sensing him and dragging him back to be questioned-- or worse.

"Guardians must never become personally involved."

"Jon," she whispered, fighting to focus so she could get the words out.

Nimble fingers undid the opening on her shirt and slid underneath the crisp fabric to caress her peaks into hardness. Sliding his hand around her back to support her, he pressed her against him while he shifted his attention to another part of her anatomy. Lazily trailing his hand along her thigh, he found her center and slowly entered, gently teasing her until she melted against him.

She couldn't keep him safe if she let this go on. Staying detached was the only way she could wield her power without her personal feelings interfering. How could she do her job if she was overcome by her emotions?

"Jon...we can't...listen to me..."

"Shhh. Relax. It'll be all right."

To keep him safe--to do her job--she had to rely on logic and not emotion. He gripped her, molding her to him so close she could feel the vibration of his heart. His rhythm was aligning with hers--beat by beat.

His energy ensnared her, pulling her in deeper and deeper. It was like being caught in wave after wave of emotion that knocked her off her feet and sent her spinning, unable to determine what was up or down.

The tumult of emotions was stronger than her ability to reason. Jon's energy engulfed her, turning her body into jelly.

Continuing his explorations, he squeezed her soft nub between his thumb and forefinger. She clenched, instinctively moving to match his pace.

"Remember the fate of your mother."

Brant had made his point by addressing the one wound that had never healed. Attacking the most vulnerable part of her because he knew--no, because Zina knew--where to inflict the most pain.

In spite of her position as a Guardian, her mother, Minona had allowed her emotions to control her when she'd contracted with Nadira's father. Rather than follow the directives of the Elders, she'd chosen a non-Guardian partner for herself.

Even that action might've been overlooked if Minona hadn't left Nova City with Nadira and gone into hiding. Driven by her desire to keep her daughter from being forced into the type of life she'd had to accept.

But Nadira's stronger Sentry energy couldn't be disguised. Minona's cousin, Zina had located them in a seaside town in the North. Untrained, Nadira had no idea how to hide her natural abilities. Making it easy for a seasoned tracker to find them.

Shuddering, she gripped Jon's arms, digging her fingers into his flesh. His emotions continued to pummel her, breaking through her reason and causing her shields to crumble.

"Remember the fate of your mother."

After that day on the beach, she never saw Minona again. She was gone. No one would tell her where.

Never forgetting the lesson, Nadira learned how to lock down her emotions. Following the example set by the Guardians who'd trained her, she chose to remain detached from her feelings.

Unable to evade her fate, Nadira accepted it. Grudgingly obeying the directives, and trying to forget the destruction of her family.

"Remember the fate of your mother."

If Zina decided to track Jon, it would only be a matter of time before she found him here. Leaving Hathor on the shuttle wouldn't be an option. Once Novacorp authorized it, he would be taken before he stepped on board.

Gritting her teeth, Nadira summoned every bit of energy she had left. She gently placed her hands on either side of Jon's face, forcing him to look at her.

"Jonathan. Please...we have to stop this."

Staring at her blankly, like he was in a daze, it took a moment for him to focus.

"What is it? Did I hurt you?"

"No...it's...it's not right. We can't do--"

"Because I'm not from Hathor or descended from the First Family or whatever the hell that is?" he asked, dropping his hands to his sides.

"Why are you angry?" Wanting to put more space between them, Nadira nudged him. But it was like trying to move a boulder. "Not being from Hathor has nothing to do with it."

"Look, I don't like mixed signals."

"Mixed signals? Damn it, Jon. I have a job to do. I'm not someone you just met at a pick-up club." Another nudge, her hands pressed against his hard abdomen. Same result, nothing.

"So you think I want to bed every woman I meet?"

"Well, don't you?" Folding her arms across her chest, she waited for a response.

Jon glared at her, gripping his towel which, by now, was barely hanging from his waist. His energy had changed all right, but his arousal hadn't dissipated. In fact, it felt even stronger than before. Maybe arguing with him was the wrong approach.

"Jonathan, I should've told you...when you were in the shower, I talked to Brant. They want to bring you back for questioning. I don't know why."

"But I don't know anything about the robbery."

"I know that. Something's going on that doesn't feel right. I need time to figure it out. But in the meantime, there's only one way to stop them from finding you. I have to use my abilities to shield you."

"Shield me? Look, I'm grateful for what you did for me last night. But I can take care of myself."

"You don't understand what they're capable of."

"If you're so good at tracking people, why can't you find Ilana and my father?"

"Some people can't be tracked as easily. It's almost impossible if they're skilled at putting up emotional shields, or they're incapacitated...or they're dead."

Jonathan staggered back and ran his hands through his slick hair. "No. He can't be dead. There has to be another reason."

Should she tell him about the remains? But what if Brant had only said that to get Jonathan to come in?

If she told him, and it wasn't true...no, she had to be sure first. She couldn't take the chance that Jonathan would do something to put himself in danger.

"Jon, do you know Mining Security Chief Mantee?"

"Sure. She's my father's second-in-command. She tried to talk me out of looking for him."

"Did she say why?"

"She said I was getting in the way." The scowl on Jonathan's face revealed more about their conversation than he was telling her. "Why do you want to know?"

"Her name came up when I talked to Brant." So, Mantee hadn't wanted him involved. She might've just been following procedure, or perhaps there was another reason for discouraging him. "I'm going to the detention building to check on the guards. They might be willing to talk."

"I'll come with you."

"No. It's best you stay here until I return," she said.

"Is there something you're not telling me?" His grey eyes were like ice. "Something else about your talk with Brant?"

If she told him, he'd run off and do something he shouldn't. She was sure of it. It wouldn't matter if he didn't have a plan. Jonathan ran on passion and impulse. That combination could be dangerous on Hathor. "No, there's nothing else. I'd better go. I'll be back as soon as I can."

Detention was only minutes away from the Administration building, but it was worlds away in appearance. There were no shimmering glass towers or bustling crowds of company personnel filling the streets.

Instead, there was one main entrance with security guards and a fence that could not be seen, but would be felt if someone tried to get through without authorization.

The detention area itself was actually a series of rooms and corridors beneath the city. It was a maze of spaces for processing and transporting offenders off-world when they were sentenced to labor in the mines.

After Nadira identified herself at the entrance, she headed to the security chief's office. Her discomfort rising as she walked past two additional security checkpoints.

Normally she tried to stay away from this place and the emotions that ran through it.

If she stayed here too long, the fear, anxiety and anger of those who had been detained would over-whelm her own feelings. Leaving her to experience them as though they were her own.

When she got to the security office, she identified herself and was admitted right away. Security Chief Duval led Nadira to a private meeting room.

"Guardian, I was surprised when they told me you were here." She waited for Nadira to sit first. "To what do I owe this visit?"

"You have two men who were involved in the attack at the Emerald Club--"

"Such an attack in the Palatine district is reprehensible, Guardian. The punishment will be most severe," Duval said, as she flicked her black shoulder-length hair away from her face.

"Yes, I know. But have they been questioned yet?"

The Chief gave her a quizzical look. "Questioned? They were processed and sent away a few hours ago."

"But the men were to be questioned by the Guardians."

"Yes, I know. I saw your request logged in the officer's report. But this morning the Sentry Leader contacted me with new instructions."

"What did he say?" Nadira asked.

"He gave authorization them to be processed. They are on their way to a mining colony. I agreed with him that lifetime hard labor was appropriate."

"Chief, has the Sentry Leader ever done this before?"

"Actually, this was the first time. But I didn't think it was my place to question him."

Of course she wouldn't have. Brant's request would've carried much more weight because of his position.

Not telling Jonathan about the remains at the mine had been the right call. They could've used Brandon's DNA profile to confirm his identity within minutes. The story had to be a lie to lure Jon in.

Reading other Guardians was difficult, though not exactly forbidden. She could take a chance and try to discover Brant's true motives. But the catch was that by doing so, she'd be vulnerable to him doing the same thing to her.

No, she couldn't take that risk. The only way to keep Jon's location secret was to build a wall of energy around them that no other Guardian could penetrate. With her stronger Sentry abilities, it would be easy. But maintaining it wouldn't be.

To create the shield, she'd have to do the one thing she'd been dreading: form an energetic connection with Jonathan.

A connection that might end up becoming permanent.

After she left the Detention area Nadira took a transport back to the Palatine district. Even with the large number of ground transports clogging the traffic lanes, she was able to get to the Emerald Club within minutes.

When she entered the lobby, Mr. Renard rushed over to her.

"Guardian! How is Mr. Keel? I have his bag here. I didn't know where to send it. Have you any word on why they attacked him? This has been most upsetting. We pride ourselves on providing safety and security for our clientele. We--"

Nadira stopped him with a wave of her hand. "Mr. Keel is recovering very well. The attackers have been dealt with."

"Yes, of course they have, Guardian. How may I help you?" he asked.

"Mr. Keel was expecting a guest to join him. Has anyone left a message or tried to check in?"

Renard frowned. "Ah, not that I can recall. But it's been so alarming in the past few hours what with security in and out. What is the name again?"

She was about to say, Ilana Travac when she remembered the alias. "It's Cintra Ansi."

"One moment." He walked back to his desk to check the hotel records. Images materialized on the surface as he tapped a short, stubby finger against the desktop. Finally he looked up. "We have no record of her, however, there was a message received for Mr. Keel."

Nadira felt her heart jump in her chest. "Who left it?"

"It is marked confidential. There's only a written message. I can't access it with the encryption, you understand." He managed a weak smile. "I wish I could assist you."

She walked over and nudged him to the side. He gasped as she pressed her hand against the glass and identified herself to the system.

"You're overriding security protocols!"

Nadira gave him a look and he backed away from her, his hands nervously clasped in front of him. Waiting for his permission would only waste more time. Right now she didn't know what she was dealing with.

Encrypted symbols flashed on the screen. Then a request: "Identify." She pressed her palm against the surface and waited for the approval. It displayed: "Approved." Then, "Unlock?" She indicated, "Yes."

The screen went blank, then displayed four words: "Message read and deleted."

"Deleted?" Nadira swiped her fingers across the desktop, paging through the displays. She knew she hadn't deleted the message. It had been there a moment ago.

"This is most unusual," Mr. Renard gasped.

"Who deleted it?" she asked. There was no response, evidently it wasn't voice activated. The message had just been there and now it wasn't. What had happened in the past few seconds?

There had to be a way to find out. Growing annoyed she went through more screens, going deeper into the system until it displayed who had accessed the message.

She stopped, her hand poised over the glass as the information she'd been searching for flashed on the screen. It read: "Message accessed, read and deleted by Jonathan Keel."

11 CONFINED

Jonathan paced the length of Nadira's small apartment. From the front door to the back bedroom was a little over 10 meters.   Hell, he had more space than that in his bedroom back on Astarte.

At least he'd found his boots halfway under the bed. But these prickly clothes were uncomfortable as hell. The t-shirt rubbed him raw and the pants irritated him in all the wrong places.

After about 10 minutes he'd been ready to strip and fling the garments into the nearest recycler. How the hell did miners wear these things?

Jon dropped down on the couch. Reaching underneath his shirt, he caught himself before he scratched the tender skin surrounding the graft. The washed-out yellow patch on his chest was a reminder of how close he'd come to being killed. Even if it never blended in to match his skin, he wasn't going to worry about it. Being burned by a stunner blast was better than being killed by one.

All he could do was sit here and wait. To make things worse, Nadira had locked the damned door. It could only be opened using her ID. That woman.

If only he could stop his body from aching whenever he thought of her. He wasn't from Hathor, so of course he wasn't good enough for her. He wasn't part of their select group.

But his mother was born here, so that had to give him some standing. Right?

Unfortunately that was the one thing he couldn't admit. But seeing how easily Nadira could read him, it was surprising he'd been able to conceal that from her.

Maybe he was getting better at putting up some emotional shields of his own. As soon as he got out of here, he was going to buy some new clothes and disappear. Let her try to find him.

Beep--beep--beep

Next to him, Nadira's tablet glowed bright blue as the shrill beeping grew more insistent. He picked it up and swiped the glass.

"Network download completed," said a computerized female voice.

The tablet was still connected to Hathor's network. He didn't have authorization to connect to it. But she did. Perfect.

"I want the Emerald Club guest services," he said.

"Guest Services connected," the computer voice responded. "Please identify."

As he'd expected, he was still checked in. Good. He placed his palm against the glass panel and identified himself to the system.

"ID accepted, Mr. Keel."

One message was waiting for him in his queue. It had to be from Ilana. But it was encrypted. He couldn't trace where she'd sent it from.

"Open the message," Jon ordered.

"Please present your ID again for access."

Ilana was taking a lot of precautions. But it didn't matter. He'd find her. Jon pressed his hand against the tablet and waited.

"ID accepted, Mr. Keel. Please wait for the message to be displayed."

Tapping his foot against the stone floor he waited. What could she possibly say to him?

Bright white letters scrolled across the cobalt blue screen.

"You're in danger. Don't stay at the hotel." Sent by Matt Bento.

He checked the date/time stamp. It'd been sent an hour after he'd checked in. By the time the message had arrived, he'd been lying unconscious in the remains of his suite with medics patching him up.

If he showed this to Nadira, she could have the Guardians bring Matt in for questioning. But how likely was that? Matt was connected and his powerful friends would protect him.

He'd have to take care of this himself.

Beneath the message, there were three buttons: Close, Save and Delete Permanently.

He chose the last option, and watched as the message disappeared.

The ride back to the apartment was taking much longer than Nadira had expected. System maintenance in the Entertainment district was tying up traffic all over the city. Now her transport was in an interminable queue of other vehicles creeping forward. In a bustling metropolis like Nova City, there was never going to be an optimum time to perform maintenance. But still, she wasn't used to waiting.

Jon had to have accessed the message. And she had a good idea of how he'd done it. She hadn't thought to tell him not to use her tablet. But she was learning quickly that when it came to Jonathan, she couldn't make assumptions. He was going to do what he wanted to, no matter what.

It turned out to be easy to check into Matt's activities in Nova City. Through the city directory Jon found details about his private club, "Whispers." Vids of prominent citizens and celebrities who attended his parties were splashed over most of the online media sites. After 30 minutes of browsing, Jon was about to stop searching when saw something.

The vid, a little over a month old according to the timestamp, was of guests arriving at a Novacorp party. Matt led the way, sauntering down a gold-trimmed red carpet followed by some company exec in a suit a couple of sizes too small. Behind them were Ilana and his father.

In flaming red hair this time, Ilana flashed a broad smile as she linked an arm with Matt. Wearing her usual body-hugging outfit, her hair flowing down her back, she stood between the men as newsers shouted questions and requests.

Not only did Ilana know Matt, but she knew his father too. Brandon never shared many details about his business trips. Now Jon knew why.

Realization was like a punch in the gut. She had to be the woman Cat saw on the mine security monitor replay.

All the tears, the stories and the sex had been to manipulate him into helping her get away. Did she have the crystal on her when they'd left on the shuttle? Or maybe she'd passed it along to an accomplice on Demeter.

There was another possibility. His father had taken the crystal and had done the robbery with her.

No. Jon could never accept that. Brandon wasn't a thief.

His father had always been there for him. Doing everything he could to help Jon open his club, even though he didn't agree with the decision. Brandon wasn't like the other self-absorbed, power-hungry company executives. He never had been.

"Abort search. Contact Matt Bento."

It took less than a minute for Matt's face to appear on the screen.

"I got your message," Jonathan announced.

"Jonathan! I'm so glad you're all right. Where are you?"

"Who sent those men to the Emerald Club?"

Matt shook his head back and forth, his eyes unfocused. "You've got to get off Hathor right away. Come over here and I'll keep you safe until the shuttle leaves. I promised Estrella--"

"Don't mention her name. If she knew what you were going to do, she'd never have contacted you."

"I'm begging you! You've got to come back to my apartment. I know what happened to Brandon."

"Tell me now!"

"No. You have to come here. I can't tell you over the network. Tell me where you are and I'll send a transport."

Matt looked like he was on the verge of crying. It might've been quite convincing if Jonathan didn't know better. "Wait there. I'll come when I can."

"Okay, Jon. I'll be here." Matt disconnected.

Going back to Matt's place would be like walking into a trap. It was a stupid thing to do. But he had no other choice.

When Nadira returned, Jonathan was slumped on the couch. He glared at her as she approached.

"You took your time getting back," he snapped.

"I thought you might want your things from the Emerald Club." She tossed his travel bag on the cushions next to him. "You used my tablet."

"So?"

"Why did you delete the message?" she asked, staring down at him.

"How do you know about it?"

"Mr. Renard saw it when I was at the hotel. You deleted it."

"It was a private message."

Reasoning with Jon was like trying to maneuver through an obstacle course. "You took a big risk doing that."

Jonathan jumped up. Gripping the drawstring of his pants, he pulled the cord so tight Nadira thought he would break it. "You left me here like a criminal in a lockup. What was I supposed to do?"

"No one knows you're staying with me. All communications on the network can be traced," Nadira shot back.

"So I'm just supposed to wait for you to protect me while I hide in your apartment?"

She needed to put up a shield between herself and the onslaught of his frustration. Everything would spiral out of control if she reacted. "What was in the message? Who sent it?"

"Tell me why I should trust you," he said.

"You should trust me because I'm protecting you. That's why you're here."

He didn't respond right away, but when he did it was with an air of resignation. "Matt sent me a warning about the attack. I talked to him. If I meet him at his place he'll tell me what happened to my father."

"Then he knows who sent the guards. Jonathan, you can't go back there. It's dangerous."

"Company security won't stop him. He's a powerful man here."

"Matt Bento doesn't have all the power on Hathor," she said.

Jon's expression softened a bit. Maybe she could get him to stop and think before he dealt with Bento.

"Let's think it through first. Then we'll decide what to do. If you still want to go to Matt's, I'll go with you."

"No."

"As I said, if you want to go to Matt's, I will be going with you. Get it?"

He shook his head, a tight smile on his lips. "Yeah, I get it."

BUZZZZZ

Nadira froze, her eyes locked with Jonathan's. It was a warning from the alert she'd set up. Designed to detect visitors based on facial recognition. It had been in place for years, though she'd never had to use it until now.

Rushing to the window nearest the door, she called out a command. "Show me the front door security monitor!"

The window darkened, then displayed a view of the sidewalk in front of the building. Security monitors regularly captured the activities around the residence. A very convenient feature to have in this case.

A shiny, grey transport vehicle was parked at the curb. And standing next to it was the person who had triggered the alert.

It was Zina.

12 BETRAYAL

Zina was leaning against the door of her private transport vehicle. A broad smile spread across her face as Nadira approached.

"I didn't realize you still lived in this district." Zina remarked. "Actually the towers of the Palatine are more befitting of your status."

"My mother and I lived in this district, as I'm sure you remember."

"I remember everything." Zina nodded, her almond-shaped eyes unusually warm. "Nadira, I was in the Sentry Leader's office when you called him today. I'm concerned."

"About what?"

"He asked you a question. You did not provide an adequate answer. Where is Jonathan Keel?"

"Why were you telling the Leader what to say?"

Zina held her hand to her mouth to suppress a laugh, but a small chuckle escaped. "Come now, Nadira. We both know he's a fool. If I didn't put words into his mouth he wouldn't have any."

"So you control Brant? Do the other Guardians know this?" she asked, keeping her face impassive under her mentor's steely gaze.

"Why were you at the Emerald Club last night?" Any pretense of friendliness evaporated as Zina took a step forward, crowding her.

"I tracked Jonathan there in case Ilana Travac showed up."

Zina was trying to force her way into Nadira's consciousness. Scanning for any crack, any weakness she could exploit. For an instant, Nadira thought about turning the tables. What better way to fight an empath than to purposely send her a flood of emotions. Overwhelm her before she could do anything to defend herself.

Had anyone been able to get the upper hand with Zina? It was tempting to give it a try. But now was not the time.

"Interesting." Zina studied her. "You tracked him up until last night, and now no one can find him."

"He was attacked. He might be hiding." Nadira felt ridiculous even saying it. That was one thing Jon would never do.

"There is something, though." Zina clasped her hands. "I find it very curious that records were accessed across the network using your ID, while at the same time you entered your ID at the Emerald Club. Guardians have many powers at their disposal, but being in two places at once is extraordinary."

"Are you tracking me?" Nadira asked. This was what she'd warned Jon about.

"How could you ask such a question, Nadira?" Zina came closer.

Backed up against the transport, Nadira's heart hammered in her chest. If her mentor picked up any awareness of Jon's energy, she'd use that to force her way in.

"You've done it before," Nadira replied.

Zina's smile faded. "Minona was my cousin, but she dishonored herself by renouncing her duty to Hathor. She made her choice."

"She made a choice that you couldn't accept." Nadira clamped down on her emotional shields. Damn it. She had to stay calm. Giving in to her feelings would allow Zina to have the advantage.

"If Ilana confided in him, she told him things that will help us to locate her. Keel must be brought in." Zina narrowed her eyes at the apartment building.

"And when I question him, there will be nothing he can hide. Nothing."

Jon was dressed and waiting when Nadira returned. Once she was in the apartment, she slumped against the door, her eyes downcast.

"Are you all right?" he asked. "Who was that woman?"

"Her name is Zina. She's my mentor."

"What happened out there?"

"She's looking for you. And she knows that someone used my ID over the network while I was at the Emerald Club."

When she looked up, her expression was strained. Instead of their usual sparkling brown, her eyes looked dull and tired. Closing the space between them, he took her into his arms.

"She can't force me to let her into the apartment. But all she has to do is have Brant give his okay and she'll send security officers here." Sighing, she relaxed against him. "There's only one way I can protect you. If you'll let me."

"What is it?"

"I'll have to create a connection between us. It'll keep her and the others from picking up your energy. I've already done it partially, but that won't be enough."

"Do what you have to do." Even as he said it, Jon wondered if he was making the right decision. Being bound to her would make it difficult--no, impossible to go off on his own.

What would it feel like to be connected to her? And how would he be able to keep his mother's secret?

The tingling started in his forehead, spreading down to his neck and chest. Pings of energy hit him like sparks from a mining drill. Shivering, he clutched Nadira tighter. Her energy melded with his own, flowing into him like molten metal.

But even as he felt the shield being assembled around them, she was maintaining a separation between their thoughts. He could feel her apprehension over Zina's visit, and something more--resentment, anger and loss. It looked to him like a deep hole that had no ending, a place she tried to cover over, but couldn't completely fill.

Now he was weightless and no longer bound by his physical body. Images formed in his mind. Nadira was a young girl at the beach. She was with a woman who she resembled, down to the same gold-flecked brown eyes.

They were standing by the sea. The woman was crying, as she clutched Nadira's hand. Zina was striding across the beach towards them. She stood before the pair, her expression triumphant. Reaching down, she touched the side of Nadira's face, then looked up at the woman and smiled.

Before he could process what he'd seen, the image disappeared. Awareness of his surroundings returned. He was back in Nadira's apartment, her head against his shoulder.

"What did I just see? Why did Zina take you from your mother?"

"My mother was a Guardian. When the Guardians discovered I had abilities, she tried to stop them from taking me." Nadira shuddered. "But they found us."

"What about the rest of your family?"

"My father, Stefan was a Novacorp security officer. His ship was lost years ago. Anyone who helped my mother to hide would've been detained or sent to the mines. I don't know what happened to them."

Strangely enough, she didn't sound upset. Instead, her words were monotone, like she was repeating a story she'd rehearsed over time.

"Maybe the rest of your family left Hathor. Why didn't your mother do that? She could've gone far away from here."

"We can't leave this planet, Jon." Nadira bristled. "No one with abilities can leave or we'll die."

"But that doesn't make sense. Who told you that?"

"I don't want to discuss it, Jonathan."

The tingling dissipated as she withdrew. But even as he felt her shutting down her emotions, there was still a small part of her that stayed connected. It remained with him as she resumed her Guardian persona and eased herself out of his embrace.

"Jonathan, if we're going to see Matt, we have to go now. Before Zina can do anything."

"What the hell does she want? Ilana didn't tell me about her plans."

"Something is going on, Jon. I don't know what it is. But if we don't leave here soon, you will be taken. And I won't be able to stop them."

Jonathan was glad the transport provided them a 360-degree view. As they trundled along the boulevard, he scanned the street, unable to shake the feeling they were being watched.

Fidgeting in his seat, he stretched out his legs, then pulled them in again. On the other end of the seat, Nadira was turned away from him, lost in her thoughts.

The car sidled up to the curb in front of Matt's building and the doors slid back.

"This is it," Jon said, as he stepped onto the marbled sidewalk.

Nadira glanced up at the tower. "Stay close."

"That will be easy."

A holo greeted them as they entered the building lobby. It was the same one who had appeared before, but this time she wore a purple and gold dress, the same color as her shoulder-length hair.

"I'm Mira, may I assist you?" she asked.

"We're here to see Matt Bento," Jon replied. "I'm Jonathan Keel, and this is my associate."

Nodding, Mira motioned towards the lifts. "He is expecting you."

The glass-enclosed lift started its ascent as soon as the doors closed. When they stopped on Matt's floor, it was deserted.

They walked down the corridor together, their footsteps barely making a sound against the cushioned floor. As they approached the apartment, the door swung open to admit them.

Matt stood at the opening. "Come in."

Inside, Jonathan looked around. It was quiet, but a feeling of uneasiness gripped him.

"Tell me what happened to my father," Jon said, not wasting time on a greeting.

"Who is this?" Matt asked, motioning to Nadira.

"She stopped the men who attacked me at the Emerald Club."

"Is she a security officer?"

The sound of heels clicking against the stone floor interrupted Jon before he could reply.

Ilana entered the room, aiming a stunner in his direction. She wore a dark blue jacket and pants. Her outfit was so severely fitted and sedate, it could've been a Novacorp-issued suit.

"Jonathan, I've missed you." She flicked her long, dark blue hair off her shoulders.

"Ilana!" Jon moved towards her, but froze when she pointed the weapon at his head.

"Are you insane? You can't discharge a weapon in here!" Matt yelled.

"You're responsible for bringing him here with a Guardian, you idiot. Don't give me orders."

"A Guardian? Shit--I can't believe this," Matt muttered, as he rubbed his hands over his face.

Next to him, Jonathan felt Nadira tense. If she could make a move before Ilana could use her weapon...

"Don't do anything you will regret," Ilana snarled, turning her attention to Nadira.

"Leave her alone!" Jon ordered.

"Always rescuing someone, aren't you? Did Matt tell you that your father planned the entire robbery and made us help him?"

"Liar!" Jon lunged forward. But before he could reach her, he heard a piercing scream.

Nadira fell to the floor, her head just missing the edge of a thick, glass table.

Racing towards her, he buckled as blasts of energy overwhelmed him. Each hit was like being zapped by bolts of electricity. Pounding him up and down his body, sending him to his knees as he searched for a way to shield himself. The room spun around him as he choked back bile.

"Ilana, stop it!" Matt cried out.

"Be quiet, you fool. It's your fault for bringing him here."

Finally the blows stopped. What did she do to him? He'd thought she'd used the stunner. Slowly, he dragged himself over to where Nadira was lying. Her eyes were closed, but she was still breathing.

"I warned her. She didn't listen," Ilana said. "Get over by the couch, Jon."

He staggered to his feet, keeping his attention on the unconscious woman on the floor. How had Ilana been able to overpower her? That shouldn't have been possible unless...unless she had the same abilities as Nadira.

"J-Jon is coming with us," Matt said, his voice shaking.

"No, he's not. We're going to your place in the North, and he's staying here. I already told you, I'm leaving in three days. When that shuttle comes in, she'd better be on it with my payment," Ilana spat. "By the way, Jon, did you know that security is looking for you? When they find you here with her, they'll punish you for attacking a Guardian."

"You're not going anywhere," Jonathan snapped. It didn't matter what she did to him at this point. He wasn't going to let her get away again.

"That's brave of you. Neither of you have any power here. I didn't even need this stunner." She shoved the weapon into her jacket pocket.

He tensed as Ilana sauntered over. She gripped his face between her hands and smashed her lips against his. Her touch was like ice. A couple of days before, he would've reacted differently. Now he was disgusted.

Grasping her arms, he tried to pull her off. But she held on, forcing her tongue between his lips.

"Get off me!" Jon thrust her away. She fell back against the couch, where she bounced down on the cushions.

In an instant Ilana was on her feet. With the wave of her hand she sent a blast of energy at him, twisting him around and sending him over a table. He landed centimeters away from the glass wall. It wouldn't take much more force to send him flying through.

"Stop it! Are you trying to kill him?" Matt's voice was a mix of anguish and anger.

With effort Jon rolled away from the wall. His body felt as heavy as the stone floor he was lying on.

"I'm done with him. Let's go," Ilana barked. "We'll call security from your aircar. They can come and get these two."

Jonathan's body was aching so much that he could barely move, much less go after them. Rolling his head over to the side, he watched the front door close behind them.

Then it was quiet.

13 FLIGHT

Nadira opened her eyes. Above her, the cream-colored ceiling swam into view. Shifting herself, she braced her hands against a nearby table and lifted her head. Bad idea. She leaned her face against the cool, glass surface of the table, and hung on, waiting for the dizziness to pass.

It was a violation for Guardians to use their powers against each other. The charge was serious enough to incur banishment--something that hadn't happened in recent memory.

Ilana couldn't have the same abilities as a Guardian. There had to be another explanation.

"Are you all right?" With a groan, Jon dragged himself over and crouched beside her. "How the hell did she do that?"

Nadira eased herself into a sitting position, resting her back against the edge of the table. "She must've used some kind of weapon or had a chemical enhancement." She'd have to wait until her head was clear before she could sort it all out.

"She didn't use a weapon," he said, his grey eyes searching hers. "It came from her--the same way you blasted those attackers."

"Her abilities aren't as strong as mine...and she hasn't been properly trained, so she's reckless. She uses all her power in her blasts." Nadira rubbed her forehead. "I tried to read her, but I couldn't get through her shields."

"If she's weaker, how could she blast you?"

"She used my abilities against me. People who are weaker can undermine someone who has stronger energy."

Jonathan helped her to her feet. Her legs were wobbly, but after a moment she was able to stand on her own.

"We have to get out of here now. They're calling security," he said.

Supported by Jon's firm arm around her shoulders, she walked out into the corridor. Within the shield she'd put around them, Jon's energy surged with anger over their encounter with Ilana.

She was glad she'd thought to put up a protection between them; otherwise his heightened emotions would be overwhelming.

"Ilana's leaving in three days. A woman's coming in on the shuttle with her payment. I don't get it. If she stole crystal from the mine, what's the payment for?"

"It's probably for robbing the mine. Maybe she stole the crystal for someone else," Nadira observed.

"They're going to Matt's house in the North. He told me he bought it from Novacorp. How far is that from here?"

"The North? A few hours. We'll have to take the boat. The autodriven transports don't go beyond the city," Nadira replied.

"An aircar will be faster. That's what they're taking."

"We'll be tracked if we hire a driver. I've never flown one," she said.

"I've never flown one either. Does that matter?" Jonathan asked, as he pushed a button for the lift.

Of course that was his answer for everything. Take the chance and figure it out later. "Yes it does matter. We could crash. We're taking the boat."

The lift doors opened. It was empty. Nadira had expected to see security officers inside.

"We won't get stopped at the boat?" Jonathan asked.

"There's less security at the ferry."

She had a clear view of the lobby through the glass doors. But there was no way to tell what was waiting for them outside the building.

"So we'll hope a boat is there when we get to the dock?" Jonathan didn't try to hide his skepticism.

"They leave regularly. Even if we have to wait, it'll be all right. Trust me."

As the lift set down at the main floor, she continued to scan the lobby for anything that seemed out of place. The tower residents were moving about as usual, and no one gave her and Jonathan a second glance.

But as they approached the glass walled entrance, she saw two officers standing outside, their faces partially covered by shiny black helmets.

"What now?" Jon asked, dropping his arm from her shoulders.

"Don't say anything," she whispered.

The entrance doors slid open, and Nadira walked out first. Composing herself, she lifted her hand and identified herself to the officers.

"Guardian," one of the officers said. "We were not aware that you had been called."

"Why are you here?" Nadira asked.

The officer held up a clear tablet in front of Jon's face. It glowed blue and flashed as his ID scrolled across the screen. "We received a report that Jonathan Keel was here. The Sentry Leader instructed us to bring him in for questioning."

"I am taking charge of him from here." Nadira summoned all her strength to put authority in her voice.

"Yes...of course, Guardian," the officer replied, sounding unsure.

At the bottom of the stairs, Nadira entered a waiting transport. She slid over and Jon climbed in.

"Take us to the ferry dock. Hurry," she instructed the autodriver.

"How far to the ferry?" Jon asked, glancing behind them.

"Approximately 15 minutes."

"They'll tell the Sentry Leader, won't they?" he asked.

"Yes. But they'll be looking for you here in the city. We'll have time before they start to search elsewhere."

How long would it take for the security officers to let the Brant know a Guardian had taken Jonathan? Staying on the transport would only make it easier for them to be stopped.

"We probably need to get off this thing," Jon suggested, as though he'd been reading her thoughts.

"You're right," Nadira said. "Autodriver, pull over to the curb and let us out."

The vehicle came to a stop in front of a busy clothing shop. Nadira climbed out first, weaving her way through the throngs of shoppers. Glancing behind her, she saw Jon darting through the crowd.

When they got to the corner, she motioned for him to follow her down the side street. "It'll be quicker if we go this way."

Keeping her awareness open, she picked up conversations, thoughts and emotions from the people she passed. Reading everyone around her was the only way to ensure they wouldn't be caught unaware by security.

If they could get to the boat without being apprehended, at least then she could rest and regain her strength.

The street fed into a tree-lined stone walkway that ran parallel to the sea. Landscaped with flowers and greenery, the waterfront stood in sharp contrast to the glass, metal and marble that dominated the city center.

"What's that over there?" Jon pointed to a long, flat white building jutting out over the water.

"It's the boat dock. That's where we're going."

"Are you sure this is a good idea? If we use our credits to get the passes, we'll be tracked," Jon said.

"I know." There was very little that could be done in Nova City that wouldn't leave a trail that someone else could follow.

Inside the terminal was calm and quiet, compared to the busy streets they'd travelled. Lit by natural light that flooded the clear ceiling, it sparkled when the sunlight hit the crystals embedded in the walls.

A holographic display showed the departures and the docks. Nadira led the way to Dock 3 where the North Country ferry was boarding.

As she'd expected, a human attendant was waiting by the entrance. Motioning for Jon to stay back, she approached the woman and smiled.

The attendant, a short woman with curly brown hair and bluish-green eyes, smiled in return. "May I help you?" she asked.

"Saludar. Par a nort? Katu?" Nadira asked as she held out her hands, palms up. Greeting her using the local dialect, with palms out as custom dictated, would let the woman know she wasn't travelling on company business. Hopefully she'd gotten the pronunciations right.

The attendant didn't answer right away. Instead she examined Nadira's hands, pausing as she noted the half-moon shaped line. If she chose to alert security, it would be easy. Just one press on the com button attached to her uniform would do it.

After a moment, the woman nodded. "Katu."

She understood. "We have to get to the North Country on the next boat and our funds are unavailable."

Reading the attendant's reactions, Nadira knew the woman was open to helping them. Guardians weren't required to provide IDs in order to travel. All she'd ever had to do was show the markings on her hand to gain admittance anywhere she wanted to go.

Unfortunately, Jonathan was another matter. Security would be alerted if he ID'd himself.

"Both of you?" she asked.

"Yes."

"The boat is in. Go up the ramp. When you get on, head to the stern. Now I have to go take care of an issue, if you'll excuse me." She walked past Nadira and headed towards the terminal entrance.

"Come on." Nadira waved at Jonathan to join her.

"What was that all about?" he asked, as they hurried up the ramp.

"I'll tell you later. Now let's get on before anyone shows up."

At the end of the ramp, they emerged into the bright sunshine. The boat was gently moving, but not enough to make her feel off balance. She sat on one of the empty benches at the stern.

"What did you say back there?" Jon asked, as he sat next to her. "Damn, these seats are hard."

"It's a language that evolved after the First Families settled here. I told her it was urgent that we get to the North. That's why she helped us." Nadira settled against the hard bench and tried to get comfortable.

"Still doesn't make sense she'd let us get on without paying." Jon stretched his legs out. "You told her we didn't have funds. We have them, we just can't access them."

"Exactly. It was my way of telling her we couldn't use an ID--without saying it directly."

"She had to figure out what you meant? Why not just say it?" Jonathan countered.

"That's not how things are done in the North. If you're too direct, people will think you're uncouth."

Jon grunted. "I'll try not to take that personally."

"You'll be fine. Just follow my lead."

"Hmmm."

"Does that mean you agree?"

"Hmmm." He leaned his head back and folded his arms across his chest.

At least she'd remembered some of the words her mother had taught her. The descendents of the First Families predated Novacorp's takeover of Hathor.

Over the generations, they'd developed ways to go around company directives when the situation called for it. That's why her mother had been assured of help when she'd left Nova City. And it was why when faced with following company rules, or helping someone with North Country roots, the attendant chose the latter.

Jon patted her knee. "You know, I'd rather sit where we can see who's getting on this boat."

Shivering, she tried to ignore the pings of energy that radiated from his touch. Even though she'd put up a barrier between them, Jonathan's energy wasn't being contained.

"The attendant won't tell anyone," she replied. "As long as you're with me, you're safe."

What was she doing? Out here on a boat, escaping the city with a fugitive? This was insane. And what made it worse, her energy, her very life force was slowly being integrated into the energy of a man she'd just met.

How long would it take before the connection between them became permanent?

14 THE NORTH

Jonathan hoped they'd get to their destination before dark. The sun was starting to set, and the two moons, Isis and Osiris were already visible in the purplish sky.

Nadira was asleep, her head on his shoulder. Shivering in the damp air, he wished he'd brought a warmer jacket. But he hadn't expected to leave the climate-controlled city.

What the hell would they do now? All they had were the clothes they were wearing. They couldn't access their credits without giving away their location.

A strange unsettled feeling came over him as saliva filled his mouth. Jonathan leaned his head back and swallowed. He'd only been on a boat once in his life, and that had been a much shorter trip than this one.

He felt like he couldn't get his balance, and with each dip his stomach pitched along with the boat.

BEEEEEP

He winced at the shrill sound of a horn. Could things get any worse on this ride?

Nadira stirred against him. "Where are we?" she asked, stifling a yawn.

"I don't know. It feels like we've been out here for hours."

BEEEEEP

Another blast of the horn. Did that thing ever stop?

"That's the signal. We'll be docking soon."

He was glad they'd managed to escape the city, but he never wanted to ride on a boat again. The only consolation was that they were closer to finding Matt and Ilana.

"You don't look so good," Nadira said, examining him with concern. "Are you all right?'

Nodding, he clamped his lips together. If he could hang on for a while longer, maybe he could make it without throwing up.

After the boat docked, they stood by the railing waiting for the other passengers to disembark. Though the boat was secured, the sound of water splashing against the hull made him to grip the rails tighter, his stomach roiling.

"Are you sure you are all right?" Nadira asked.

"I'm fine. Let's get off this thing." He hated being on boats. Desperate to get back on solid ground, he plodded towards the gangway.

He'd hoped by the time his feet touched the stone tiled walkway, he'd feel better. But with each step, it felt like the ground was moving.

"Now we have to find Matt's house," she said.

"We could ask someone. There were a lot of people on the boat." Even as he said it, he knew it wasn't likely. The passengers filing past them, in green and blue coveralls, were most likely mine workers. Some of them had travel bags slung across their bodies; perhaps they were returning from R&R in the city.

She pointed to the kiosk at the end of the walkway. "We'll check the public directory."

"If he's hiding Ilana there, I doubt it's a place he wants a lot of people to know about," Jon said.

The kiosk wasn't online and no holo greeted them when they approached. It figured that there wouldn't be any conveniences out in the middle of nowhere.

"Can't you track Matt?" Jonathan asked.

"I've been trying. I thought something would look familiar." She indicated an empty patch of sand to the left of the kiosk. "There used to be a big house there."

All he could see, besides the sand and beach grass, were several rectangular-shaped houses along the shore. Other than that, it looked pretty desolate. He couldn't imagine why anyone would come to this place, much less live here.

"It's been years. Maybe you're mistaken," he said, as he wiped away sand that had blown in his face.

"No. I'm sure of it. It was over there."

A light came on in one of the houses to their right. Through the long narrow window on the lower level, he could see someone moving around. It looked a hell of a lot more inviting than standing out here being pelted by sand.

"Maybe someone in that house can help us. The local people might know where we can find Matt's," he suggested.

"I don't know. They might call security."

"We can't just stand around thinking." They had to do something, and he was running out of ideas.

"Perhaps if we'd figured things out first, we wouldn't be standing around." Nadira bristled.

"I wanted to take the aircar. At least then we would've been here sooner and looked around in the daylight." Was she blaming him for this?

"You couldn't fly one!" She snapped.

"It would've been better than riding on a boat for hours!"

"You said you knew where Matt's house was. So where is it?" Nadira asked, motioning around her.

"I said it was in the North. You're from here. Why don't you know?" he retorted.

"Just because I'm from here doesn't mean I know where his house is!"

"And if you'd blasted Ilana back at Matt's, we wouldn't be stuck out here chasing them!"

As soon as he said it, he regretted it. If she got pissed, she might either blast him or leave him out here to figure things out on his own.

Neither of those options would be good for him.

"Look, I'm sorry," he began. "I didn't mean to say--"

"Are you lost?"

Jonathan froze, who was that? Looking in the direction of the voice, he saw a man standing on the stairs of the lighted house. He waved to them to come over.

"It's getting colder. Maybe he can help us find out where Matt's place is." He pulled his jacket tighter, though there wasn't much excess fabric to pull.

Nadira didn't respond, in fact she didn't even look at him.

He sighed. With night coming and the temperature dropping, he had no interest in wandering around without a destination.

She didn't protest when he led her down the walkway and over to the house. Guided by the light of the moons, it was easy to find a path through the velvety fronds of beach grass.

15 No More Rules

"You're here from the city, aren't you?" the man asked as he stepped aside to let them enter the house. "My name is Jason. I heard you outside. It sounded as though you needed assistance."

"Yes we sure could," Jon said as he led the way inside. The foyer was darkened, but bright light flooded in from the connecting room. "I'm Jon and this is Nadira."

He wondered if giving their names was a smart thing to do. But it wasn't likely anyone would be looking for them out here. "We came to visit a friend of mine, Matt Bento. We wanted to surprise him, but the directory out there isn't working and we're not sure where the house is."

"The name is not familiar to me. Come in." Jason motioned for them to follow him.

The dining room had a large wooden table that could seat at least 10 people, and colorful woven hangings on the walls. Jonathan was surprised that the furnishings were as modern as he would've found in his own apartment. He'd been expecting something a lot more rustic.

A three-quarter wall divided the room, with an opening at one end providing access to the other side. He could hear people moving about and the aroma of food being prepared.

"I manage this guest house. Company managers usually stay here during the season, but it's quiet now." Jason rubbed his hands against the long, blue apron he wore over his shirt and pants. "You work for the company, don't you? Are you on holiday?"

Short and compact, Jason's shirtsleeves were rolled up, revealing his sinewy arms. Wisps of grey hair on the sides of his head kept him from being completely bald. Except for his height and his cheerful expression, he reminded Jonathan of the Sentry Leader, Brant.

Jonathan waited for Nadira to sit before he joined her at the table. "We're just visiting for a few days."

"I used to live in the North Country many years ago. Wasn't there a big house out there on the other side of the kiosk?" Nadira asked.

HATHOR LEGACY: OUTCAST

"Oh, that has been gone for many years." Jason
stroked his chin. "It was destroyed oh...about...yes, almost 20 years ago."

"What happened?" Nadira asked.

"It was a fire." Jason's smile faded.

The crash of a metal object hitting the floor reverberated from the other side of the wall. Jason closed
his eyes in exasperation, quickly forcing a smile to his
lips. "There is a small problem in the kitchen." He hurried to other side of the dividing wall.

"What's so important about that house? Did you
live there?" Jon asked.

"No."

Instead of elaborating, she stared straight ahead,
her lips tight. So, she was still angry. Well, she'd have
to get past it.

"Did you check him out with your powers? Is he
okay?" Jason seemed friendly, but it was best to be
sure.

"Yes, I used my 'powers' to read him when we
walked in," she snapped.

"Look, we can't use our credits or we'll be identified. I'm not in the mood to wander around tonight. If
you talk to him in that dialect, he might help us out."

He did want to keep going. But, after what Ilana
had done to both of them, he had to admit that rushing to confront her again without a plan would be in-
credibly stupid.

Their host returned, his easygoing manner back in place. "New workers make mistakes at times. All is well now. Would you like me to try to locate your friend?"

Nadira held up her left hand. "Jason, can we stay here tonight? It is a private matter. Katu?"

Jason's smile grew wider, causing creases to cut across his forehead. "Yes, of course. You are welcome, Guardian. Please honor me by staying. Our largest room on the top floor is quite comfortable."

"Thank you. Perhaps we can have something to eat."

"Yes, of course! I will see about the meal." Jason clasped his hands together and headed back to the kitchen.

A moment later Jon heard him shouting instructions to the workers as the sounds of activity increased. In spite of his earlier nausea, Jon's stomach growled as he caught a whiff of a pleasing smell from the kitchen.

"All you have to do is ask and it's done? I'm impressed."

Nadira looked into his eyes, her brown ones intense and unwavering, a small smile on her lips. She was used to giving commands and being obeyed. But so was he.

"Here we are." Carrying a pitcher and two cups, Jason emerged, followed by a younger man and woman carrying trays of food. "These are my assistants, Jare and Lora. So far tonight you're our only guests, so you will get our best."

"Grasi," Nadira said.

"Thanks. This is a nice house." Barely waiting for the woman to set it down, Jonathan reached for one of the platters. The steaming mix of vegetables and meat was still sizzling, making his mouth water. He didn't recognize any of the dishes, but it didn't matter. He was hungry.

"The company owns most of the houses facing the sea. I've been managing this one for several years. Many people come here on holiday from the city."

"Why?" Jon asked, ignoring the sharp look Nadira gave him. Though he'd grown up in a home overlooking the sea, he'd never understood the attraction.

"Ah, I see you prefer a faster pace," Jason observed, a hint of amusement in his bluish-green eyes. "Well, we will try to make you comfortable while you are here."

A couple of hours later, Jason led them to the upstairs bedroom. Not only was the room large, it had a huge bed that sat on an ornately carved platform. A dark blue, plush couch wrapped around the opposite wall. Above it, the window spanned the wall, from one end to the other.

From where he was standing by the bed, Jonathan could look out and see the ocean waves shimmering in the golden light of the moons.

Jason pulled back the velvety bed covers and fluffed the long pillow. "I'm sorry I could not locate Matt Bento's home for you."

"We'll see what we can find out tomorrow." Jonathan took off his jacket and tossed it on the bed.

"Fine. Be rested." Jason nodded at them and left the room.

"Which side do you want?"

Nadira didn't respond as she stood at the foot of the bed, staring out at the sea.

"Something wrong?" he asked.

"I'm fine."

Still tight-lipped. What was it going to take for her to stop being angry at him?

"Nadira, I'm sorry about the things I said out there."

"Are you?"

"Look, you're right. We need to think first before we do anything else. From now on, I'll listen. I promise."

"Jon, we should get some rest. We'll need it." She went to the other side of the bed and began undressing.

He pulled off his shirt, kicked off his boots, then added his pants and underwear to the pile. Climbing into bed, he saw that Nadira was still undressing.

Neatly folding her jacket and pants, she laid them on a nearby chair. Her shirt came next. Then she was down to her underwear, just as she had been that morning back in her apartment. Her sleeveless tank top hugged her rounded breasts and stopped above her midriff. Below that, all she had on was a triangle of sapphire-colored fabric.

Suppressing a groan he thought about the last time she'd allowed him to touch her there. It'd nearly driven him crazy.

Nadira slid under the covers next to him but remained on her side of the bed.

"Why don't you move over?" he asked. "I won't do anything I shouldn't."

To his surprise, she moved close enough for him to put his arm around her waist.

"That's better, isn't it?"

"Yes," she replied.

"So you haven't been in the North since you left with Zina?" He wasn't sure if this was the subject to bring up right now. But he was curious.

"No, I haven't. Being back here doesn't feel the same. I thought it would."

"There's something I don't understand. When we were back at your place, how was I able to see your memory of Zina taking you from your mother?"

Nadira didn't say anything. All he heard was her deep breathing, then a sigh.

"I'm not sure, Jon. Maybe it's our connection."

All this time he'd assumed that she'd purposely stayed open to him. But she'd had no control over it.

"Why didn't your mother want you to become a Guardian? Do you know where she is now?"

She shifted her body away from him. "Too many questions, Jonathan, and I don't have the answers right now."

"I'm sorry. Don't move away. It's cold. The closer you are the warmer we'll both be."

She laughed. It was a small sound, like she had to force it. But she did move close enough to press the length of her body against his.

As much as he enjoyed it, it would be torture to continue to start something that couldn't be finished. A little foreplay wasn't so bad, but at some point they had to get to the destination.

"Your skin isn't itching anymore?" she asked.

He'd almost forgotten about the fake skin. "Guess it's healing," he replied. "Just like you said it would."

"Lights 0%," she called out. The ceiling lights went dark, leaving the room lit only by moonlight. "That's because I'm always right."

He closed his eyes, enjoying the feeling of her presence so close to him in the warm, comfortable bed. Always right? He'd have to wait until morning to give her an answer.

Hours later Jonathan woke up with a start. He'd been dreaming that he was running. But he must've actually thought he was running, because his body had jerked and he'd woken himself up.

"Can't sleep?" Nadira asked.

"Did I wake you?"

"I've been awake for a while. It's hard to relax."

Nadira draped her leg across his, setting his nerve endings on fire. What was she doing? He sighed so deeply he startled himself.

"Are you all right?" she asked.

"Why do you keep asking that?"

"You sounded like something was hurting."

"Nothing's hurting." She had to know why he was reacting the way he was. Or maybe she was deliberately teasing him. If so, he had a way to turn the tables. He reached under the covers and rested his hand on her bare thigh.

"What are you doing?" she asked.

"What do you mean?"

"Your hand. Why is your hand there?" Nadira asked. "And now what are you doing?"

His hand was now curved around her backside, and while it was there he was going to make the best of it.

"Does this bother you?" he asked, kneading her hip. He might as well keep going until she told him otherwise. No matter what happened, he didn't expect to have a restful night.

"No, it doesn't."

Maybe the situation was improving. She didn't seem uncomfortable. But how far would she allow things to go?

"Nadira, what is it? You can't be with someone who's not a Guardian? Are there rules?"

He felt silly for asking, but he did wonder. Guardian rules for sex: what not to do and who not to do it with.

"It's hard to experience my own emotions as well as someone else's. Staying in control of my energy is important. If I don't, I won't be able to focus it properly."

"But what does that have to do with sex?"

She laughed. "Everything is energy, Jon. It's all connected. Do you understand?"

"So if you lose control you could blast me?" he asked, hoping she could tell he wasn't entirely serious.

"No. It's different."

"That's good to know." He chuckled.

"What we're feeling right now...the arousal we're feeling...it's probably only because I'm shielding you."

"I doubt that. And I don't think you believe it either," he said, as he continued to caress her. "It doesn't matter to you that I'm not a Guardian?"

"It doesn't."

"Do you trust me?" he asked, his heart racing.

It took a few moments for her to answer, but finally she did. "Yes," she whispered.

Without hesitation he pressed his lips against hers. She returned his kiss, opening her mouth and giving way to his probing tongue.

Guiding her so that she was on her back, he continued kissing, playing, and biting, while he lost himself in the vibration from the moans that escaped her lips. She'd driven him to distraction since that first chase, and now it was his turn.

Anxious to remove any barriers between them, he gently lifted up her top and pulled it over her head, discarding it to join his clothing on the floor. Trailing kisses down her body, he captured her full breasts, running his hands over them, grasping and gently squeezing. He found her nipples, enjoying her reactions as he caressed them into hardness.

Encouraged by her soft sighs, he ran his hand across her stomach, then down to that triangle of fabric that had caused him so much consternation. Pushing back the fabric, he found her nub and ran his thumb over it, squeezing it between his thumb and fingers. She tensed, her breathing deep and ragged.

"Do you want me to stop?" He had to ask, to be sure she was still with him.

"No."

Lingering over her for a moment more, he hugged her to him. Feeling her body pulsing against him, tingling in anticipation, enjoying the power he had over her reactions.

Jon moved back down her body, planting kisses as he went, deliberately making his progress last as long as possible. With each contact of his lips and tongue against her skin, he could feel her emotions churning within her.

Though he was taking his time with her, his own desires were setting him on fire. With one quick pull, he was able to free her from the sapphire blue triangle of fabric. Positioning himself at her moist opening, he teased her with his tongue, driving her until her moans became cries, and she was writhing under his firm grip. He knew she craved release but he wasn't going to let her have it just yet.

Continuing to tease her, he flicked his tongue over the sensitive mound, gently nipping and sucking. By remaining open to him, she was allowing Jon to experience her desires in addition to feeling his own.

Her moans grew louder and deeper, vibrating within him, driving him to the edge. As much as he delighted in pleasuring her this way, he also wanted more. But first, he'd let her have what she was desperate for.

It only took a moment more to coax her to the brink. As her body tensed, his did too. He gripped her tighter, holding on to her as she trembled and pulsed, almost sending him over the edge. After a long, deep sigh she relaxed against the bed cushions, her body still.

Unable to hold back any longer, he positioned himself, one hand under her hips. He eased into her slowly, waiting for any sign of her discomfort. But there was no resistance. Instead she pressed her legs against him, her hands braced on his shoulders.

Being inside her was almost enough to send him to the point of exploding, but he forced himself to gently pull back, then ease in again. Her slickness made his movements easy; her tightness surrounded him, co-cooning him, accommodating him.

Her emotions flooded him to the point where he wasn't sure which were hers and which were his. All he knew was that he was completely engulfed, and yet it wasn't like drowning. It was a joining between them, connecting him to her even more than he'd been before.

With a loud cry he released himself, and was instantly struck by an energy rebound that left him gasping. As his body jerked he felt Nadira's arms wrap around him, holding him close as he felt a second and third rebound hit him. Through their connection he felt her body reacting as well. Their combined energy moved between them, each time with less force, like an echo that eventually faded and left them spent.

With a groan he rolled onto his back, his arms and legs outstretched, his sweat-drenched skin sticking to the bed covers. As he returned to awareness, he felt Nadira's presence next to him. Touching her, he immediately withdrew as the connection between his fingertips and her skin lit up his nerve endings.

Desperate for contact, he braved the shocks and satisfied himself with leaning his head against hers on the pillow.

"I've never felt anything like that," he said, his voice sounding like it was coming from far away.

"Neither have I," she whispered.

"We've broken all the rules, haven't we?"

She turned to him, her forehead touching his. "There are no rules, Jon. Not any more."

16 No Going Back

When Nadira woke, sunshine was pouring through the windows, lighting up the room in a bright golden glow. She leaned on her elbows, straining to look out at the sapphire sea. Foamy white caps bubbled up, then dissolved with the movement of the waves.

Jonathan was still asleep, his back to her. Resisting the urge to touch him, she slid out of bed and padded into the adjoining shower area. There was one long shower, tiled in sapphire and emerald that sparkled in the sunlight. At the end, a clear glass wall gave her a view of the gardens at the rear of the house.

Drops of water hit the top of her head as soon as she stepped into the shower enclosure. She pressed the temperature indicator on the wall, setting it for a hot shower. The water washed over her, sending rivulets down her body, mixing with a creamy soap that filled the room with the smell of spicy flowers.

As she rubbed it over her skin, she thought of Jon touching her, pleasuring her in a way that she'd never experienced before.

Zina had discouraged her from forging relationships with anyone who wasn't a Guardian. No doubt her mentor wanted to keep her from doing the same thing her mother had done.

But intimacy with other Guardians had never sated her. They were always too focused on shielding themselves, reluctant to let anyone else in, even for sex.

She turned off the water and activated the body dryer. The warm air flowed over her, enveloping her in a slightly moist cocoon. After she finished preparing herself for the day, she returned to the bedroom to get dressed.

Jon was still asleep, so she quietly slipped out of the room and headed downstairs. Jason was sitting at the dining table reading something on his tablet while he drank his coffee.

"I haven't smelled coffee like that in years," she said, sitting down across from him. "Could I have some?"

"Ah yes. Smells good, doesn't it?" He pushed his chair back and walked into the kitchen, returning a few moments later with a cup. "The beans are grown a few kilometers from here."

"Grasi." Nadira took the cup from him and sipped the steaming hot beverage. She rarely drank coffee at home. But it was hard to resist something that reminded her of her childhood.

Jason rested his arms on the tabletop. "I've had very few Guardians visit this house. When they do come, they don't use our language. They think it's beneath them. Who taught you those words?"

She was taken aback by his directness. "My mother taught me."

"She was from the North?" He rubbed his balding head, his large hand pausing to scratch the tip of his ear. "Your pardon, I'm sure I'm asking too much. But when you mentioned the house by the kiosk, it raised questions in my mind."

"Yes. We left the city when I was eight years old and stayed in the North for a while." Not sure how much to reveal to him, she chose her words carefully. "I had family here."

"So that is when your gift developed?" He nodded, taking a sip of coffee. "People in the North have the strongest abilities. That's why Guardians come here most often when they are looking for people to train."

"Why is that true, Jason? I've never heard that before."

"This planet is still a work in progress, even after generations. When Hathor was being terraformed, the people from Earth settled in the North. Then Novacorp came, and the West became populated. The

people here in the North Country are the true descendants of the First Families. That is why this gift came
to us."

He paused to take another sip before continuing.
"For Novacorp, the value of the Guardians is that they
have a ready-made security force with extraordinary
powers. Once the company recognized that, our people
accepted that this was not something to be feared."

"Jason, when they discovered my abilities, the
Guardians wanted my mother to give me to them for
training. That's why she left Nova City and came
here."

Even as she said it, Nadira felt discomfort. Never
had she heard anyone call her power a gift. If it was,
why hadn't her mother embraced it?

"Ah, I see. Not every parent is pleased to have a
child with abilities." A frown passed over his face, then
quickly disappeared. "I also have abilities, though they
were never strong enough to be developed. Would you
show me your hand again?"

Nadira thrust her hands out, palms up. "I'm sorry. I
should've done this as soon as we were introduced."

"No bother. That's an old custom. It's of little con-
sequence these days." Jason examined her hands, running his finger over the half-moon line in her palm.
"How strong are you? This line is very deep."

"I'm a Sentry."

He looked up at her, his mouth open. "Are you really? There have not been many. Maybe three or four are born in a generation. You are favored."

Was she? It was hard to feel that way considering what it had cost her.

"The custom of showing your palms came from the days when people misunderstood what the powers were. It was done to show that you didn't have the markings and were not a threat." He released her hands.

"I wasn't taught that during my training, Jason."

"That is because the history you were taught is according to Novacorp. When they took over, they took all our historical records into their possession." He sighed, his eyes downcast. "Perhaps I should not say this, but the house you asked about was destroyed by Guardians.

"They destroyed it? Why?"

"At times people had hidden from the Guardians in that house. I suppose when it was discovered, they were angry." He cradled the cup in his hands.

"Why are you telling me this, Jason?"

"If you were like the other Guardians I've met, I would not have said anything." Jason's fingers tensed as he gripped his cup. "But I wanted to give you the truth. Perhaps you can look for your family while you are here."

"That's in the past now. I can't go back." Nadira felt her hand trembling as she finished her coffee. This wasn't what she wanted to talk about right now.

"Well, you are back, aren't you? This may be an opportunity."

"You said the houses by the shore were built by Novacorp," she remarked.

"Yes. About 10 years ago. I was working on my family's farm and I found that it was not for me." He chuckled. "Here I can live near the sea, maintain the house and entertain visitors when they come. I have no complaints."

"Is there anywhere that isn't controlled by Novacorp, Jason? Wouldn't you like to experience that?"

He looked off to the side, thinking of an answer. It came quicker than Nadira expected. "Is there such a place? Neither of us can leave Hathor, so it's best to accept what we can't change." Jason pointed to her cup. "Do you want more?"

"No, thank you."

"That coffee smells good!" Jonathan padded across the floor in his bare feet, his shirt open and half tucked into his pants.

"Perhaps you should finish dressing," Nadira smirked.

"I'm sure you're both hungry," Jason said, as he got up from the table. "My assistants have not arrived yet.

I'll go prepare food." With a quick nod to Nadira, he picked up his tablet and headed into the kitchen.

After he sat down next to her, he leaned over to plant a kiss on her mouth. "I'm still knocked out from last night."

She motioned towards the kitchen. "We're not alone."

"He knows we slept in the same bed," Jonathan said. "What did he think we were doing up there, discussing speed of light travel?'

"Jon, we have to focus."

"That's what I'm doing." This time he moved in for a lingering kiss that left her breathless.

"Jonathan!" Pulling away from him wasn't as easy as she'd hoped, especially not with her heart racing.

"It's a bit late to play hard to get." He grinned at her. "Hey, where's Jason's tablet?"

"He took it with him."

"Why?" Jon paused, his attention on the dividing wall. "Wait--I hear him talking to someone."

Nadira heard it too, but it sounded like a woman's voice. No, he wouldn't betray them. Or had she misjudged?

"I'd better go check." Jon headed over and almost bumped into Jason as he rushed out of the kitchen.

"You have to see this!" He rushed over and handed the tablet to Nadira. "There's an alert."

Taking it from him, she stared at the still image on the screen.

Two faces were displayed side-by-side. On the left was a man with short, curly brown hair, strewn with strands of grey. His features were familiar: squared face, rough-hewn with a hint of stubble. It was an older version of Jonathan except with brown eyes.

Underneath his picture flashed the words, "Demeter CEO Presumed Dead" in bright red. On the right was a picture of Jonathan.

"There is a security alert for the apprehension of Jonathan Keel for questioning in this matter. Do not approach. Contact security if this individual IDs himself in your vicinity. This has been a message from Novacorp Security," the computerized voice intoned.

"What the hell?" Jon reached over and snatched the tablet out of Nadira's hands.

"Jonathan, we knew this was going to happen--" Nadira began.

"But you didn't mention the 'Demeter CEO presumed dead' part!"

Nadira tensed. "Jon, I'm sure it's a mistake. They just haven't found him yet, that's all."

If Jonathan found out that she'd known about the remains, what would he think of her?

"They claim Mr. Keel escaped from the city because he is purposely withholding information from the authorities," Jason said, as he studied Jonathan. "But I know that a Guardian would not protect anyone who was a criminal."

His words reassured her, though it was surprising that he trusted her judgment with so little knowledge of her motives. "If someone wanted to travel in the North and maintain their privacy, how difficult would that be?" she asked.

"Not difficult, though it would be wise to travel by private transport, rather than to use the public vehicles."

Sure it would be a lot better. But they didn't have one. There had to be a quick way to find out where Matt's house was located.

"Jason, is there a public com nearby?" Jonathan asked.

"Yes. It's about thirty minutes away by transport. When my assistants arrive, I'll have one of them take you over there. They'll be here very soon."

"We can go there to access the directory and find Matt's house," Nadira said.

"I know. I'll take care of it. You wait here."

"Jon, I don't think we should separate. If security finds you, they'll take you to detention."

"If I'm detained, I don't want you to get stopped with me. Just tell them you didn't have a choice. I forced you into helping me escape."

She almost laughed at his suggestion. "I didn't have a choice?"

"No, you didn't," he said. "We're connected now, and there's no going back."

As soon as Jason's assistant, Lora arrived at the house, Jason had her drive Jon to the com station. Taller than Jason, she had dark blue eyes and matching hair that she wore in thin, long braids.

Most importantly she was friendly enough, and she didn't ask too many questions.

As far as he was concerned, the view from the road was just as uninteresting as the beachfront. One sand dune looked just like another, and the boxy, rectangular houses all had the same drab, grey or brown exterior.

"Is it always this quiet?" Jon asked, as he watched the scenery go by.

"The season hasn't started yet. When it does, there will be more visitors," Lora replied, not taking her attention from the road.

"You do a lot of different jobs, don't you?"

"Yes, I'm learning from Jason. I hope to manage a house when I've learned enough."

"That's good," he said, not sure how else to respond. Managing a house by the shore was not his idea of an exciting profession, but Lora seemed happy with it.

What if Nadira had never been discovered by the Guardians? Would she have been satisfied with this type of life? Working in a guest house or in a manufacturing complex? He doubted it.

Thirty minutes later, Lora steered the transport into a large, open area where several other vehicles and cycles were parked.

"Here we are," she said.

"I'll be right back." Jon climbed out and strode over to the L-shaped, stone building in front of them.

The public communications center was also a transport terminal, in addition to a food market and a gathering place. A sign pointed him to his first destination: the directory. It was a long wall of frosted glass right across from the food stalls.

As soon as he walked up, a woman's face appeared on the surface, her purple eyes shimmering.

"Hello, my name is Sila. How may I help you?"

"I need a location search for properties owned by Matt Bento in the North Country." Jason had already done this search the night before. But Jonathan had to be sure.

"There is no known location for that individual in the North Country," she said, flashing a set of extremely white teeth.

Maybe there was a way to narrow things down. "Give me a list of the private houses in the North, excluding farms."

"I'm sorry. I'll need an additional cross reference. Those results will create an overflow."

"Sila, how large is the North Country?

"The North Country, also known as Sector 3, covers approximately 321,868.2 kilometers and contains the largest concentration of farm land, manufacturing plants, and developed shoreline than any other area on the Novacorp HQ planet. The planet, also known as, Hathor was discovered by astronomers at the Space Administration in the solar year 2234 and--"

"Stop! That's enough." There was no way they were going to find Matt's house without a definitive location.

"How would I find somebody if I didn't know where to look?"

"Are they lost?"

At first he thought she was joking. "I'm lost."

"Oh! Well, in that case, please inform me where you are now."

"That's what I'm asking you!"

Sila's eyes rolled back and forth. She was either thinking or on the verge of a system failure. "You are in the 7th District, Public Communications Station Four. Where would you like to be?"

"Wait. The North is divided into districts?"

"Of course, isn't everything?"

Now he was sure she was joking. Just what he needed, a computer with a sense of humor.

A search by district would be a hell of a lot easier. Jon was about to make another request when out of the corner of his eye, he saw a woman in a dark uniform heading towards the food stalls. Shit. It was time to break this off.

"End the query, Sila."

"Query ended. Have a wonderful day!" She flashed one last smile before her image disappeared.

Keeping an eye out for the security officer, Jon headed to the com booths. Located away from the busy food stalls, the coms were tucked away in a corner of the building.

Following the instructions on the screen, he requested his connection. At least his ID wasn't required on the public com. That would keep security from tracking him.

It took several moments to route the call to Cat's com ID. Interplanetary communication wasn't always quick or efficient. He knew he was taking a chance by waiting, especially with the officer just steps away.

"Please wait" continued to scroll across the screen. What if she didn't answer?

Just when he was about to break off the call, Cat's face appeared. Unfortunately the layer of finger smudges on the screen made her image look like it was out of focus.

"Jonathan!"

"Hello, Cat," he said.

"Where the hell are you, you little shit? You disobeyed me and you took that woman with you!"

So much had happened; he'd forgotten that Cat would still be angry at him for leaving. "There's no time to talk about that now. Did you know there's an alert out saying--"

"When I saw Ilana Travac's name on the shuttle passenger list, I knew you were responsible. Jonathan, what were you thinking to take up with that slag?"

"I get it! I was wrong. Look, there's an alert out about my father. What the hell is going on?"

She paused, a strained look on her face. "We found remains. I'm sorry, Jonathan. It's not confirmed, but...but we have to accept that Brandon was probably killed in the explosion."

Her words jolted him. "No. That can't be true. "How long have you known?"

"I was required to report it to headquarters. Brandon has a partial ownership in the mine. I made a report to company security the day after your shuttle arrived."

Jonathan slumped in his chair. That was the day he'd been in Nadira's apartment recovering. The same day she'd talked to the Guardian Sentry Leader. So she had to have known.

"How about my mother and sisters?"

"Your family is worried about you, Jonathan. You have to come home now. Don't wait for the company shuttle. I can have a private one ready to bring you to Astarte. Just tell me where you are."

She was right. But if he left, Ilana would get away.

"I know who's responsible. If I leave now, they'll never find her."

"Look, I'm trying to protect you."

"I already have the protection I need, Cat."

"Do you mean that Guardian you're running around with?" She scowled at him. "First Ilana, and now this woman. You've been manipulated and you don't even know it."

"Wait a minute--how do you know I'm with a Guardian?"

"I've taken enough of your crap. I'll have you picked up and detained."

"Answer me!" Jon demanded.

Cat shot him a look of contempt. "When you get back, you'll never leave Astarte again without my permission. And after this stupid shit you've pulled, you'll never get it."

The screen blanked out.

"Damn it!" He brought his fist down so hard he thought the screen would break. Jon glanced around, luckily the booths nearby were empty.

Should he contact his mother and ask her what was happening there? As much as he wanted to, he couldn't take the chance. It was best to leave now.

It was warmer outside than when he'd first gone in. Jonathan pulled his jacket off and climbed into the transport.

"Lora, take me back to the house," he said.

"Yes, of course. Are you all right?"

"I'm fine." His head was pounding and he felt like throwing up. "Just get me back there as soon as you can."

"Yes, sir."

His father was dead. And Nadira had known about it. Why hadn't she told him?

17 FRAGILE

When Lora pulled up behind the house, Jonathan barely waited for her to stop before he hopped out. During the ride, he'd replayed every conversation with Nadira in his mind--every look, every touch--had it all been done to break down his resistance? Just as Ilana had done.

And they both had the same powers.

He trudged along the gravel path leading from the parking area to the front door. With each step, he felt like he was slogging through thick mud. Had he been that much of a fool?

Turning the corner, he stopped in his tracks. Nadira was standing on the front stairs looking out at the sea. Her arms crossed, her short dark hair ruffled by the breeze. What was she thinking? If only he could tell. But his ability to see her thoughts came and went without his control.

"What happened?" she asked, still gazing at the water.

"How did you know I was here?" Stupid question. Would he ever get used to her powers?

She turned to face him, her eyes wet. "I felt it. Something's wrong. Isn't it?"

"Let's talk over there."

Purple fronds of beach grass shot up through the slate grey sand. He led the way, pulling back the slender shafts as they tramped down to the water's edge.

Stopping at a point just above the water line, he watched as the waves rolled onto the shore, then retreated, leaving bubbling foam in their wake.

"What is it?" she asked.

"While I was at the com station I called Cat Mantee."

"The Mine Security Chief? You shouldn't have done that. What if she reports your location to security?"

"I asked her about my father."

Nadira took a step towards him. "There's something more."

Tingling spread across his face and down over his chest and arms. What the hell? She was reading him.

"Cat said they found my father's remains the day after I arrived. She reported it to the Guardians." He braced himself before continuing. "That was the day I was at your apartment. The same day you talked to the Sentry Leader. He told you, didn't he?"

"Jonathan, I didn't believe him. I didn't trust what he was saying."

"But you should've told me! You didn't have the right to decide what I needed to know."

"You don't understand, Jon. Zina was telling Brant what to say. They have their own agenda."

"Everyone has an agenda, Nadira. Even you."

"What are you saying? Do you think I did all of this to betray you?" she asked. "I'll probably be banished for what I've done."

"You were the one I thought I could trust. My father's been dead all this time, and you never told me."

The only way he could keep himself clear was to leave now. If he stayed, if he listened to her, he might change his mind.

"I wasn't deliberately hiding anything, Jon. I wanted to protect you. That's why I brought you to my apartment and that's why I'm here now."

After what had happened between them, withdrawing from her wouldn't be easy. But he could do it.

Hunching his shoulders against the icy sea air, he turned away from her.

"Jonathan!"

"Go back to the city. I'll be okay."

"I'm not leaving. We're going to find Ilana together."

"I don't need your help." Was she following him? It didn't matter. From now on he'd focus on finding Ilana and Matt and shove everything else out of his mind.

Nadira stood by the water's edge, watching as Jonathan headed back up the path. He ran up the stairs and went inside, the door slamming shut behind him.

Why couldn't he understand she'd only wanted to protect him?

"My pardon!" Jason rushed down the path, his apron flapping. "Jon said he's leaving to go find your friend, Matt Bento. Did something happen?"

"We had a difference of opinion."

Jason picked his way through the grass and joined her by the waterline. "He refused to have Lora take him back to the com station. He's a CEO's son. I'm concerned about him walking about without an escort."

"Is it so dangerous here?"

He seemed shocked by the question. "Of course not. No one would dare to harm him, but still, he should receive a certain courtesy."

Jason certainly was a good fit for his role. Though she wasn't sure if he really did feel the executive class deserved more consideration, or if he wanted to stay on the good side of those in power.

"I'm not leaving until we have a plan," Nadira said. "So he's not going anywhere either."

"Then there is no problem between you? He seems agitated." Jason glanced back towards the house. "Sometimes relations are difficult for Guardians. And, forgive me for mentioning it, but it is obvious that there are relations between you."

It should've been more than obvious by now. "That's something that should remain private, Jason."

"You are not the first Guardian to come here with that request. There are times when discretion is the better choice." He clasped his hands over his apron. "I'm aware that relations with Fragiles are not encouraged. At first I thought perhaps that was why you came here and I--"

"What--what are you saying?" Nadira held out her hand to stop him from continuing. "Fragiles?"

Jason leaned closer, like he was sharing a confidence. "Traditionally people from the North have little affection for off-worlders, particularly the ones who are connected to Novacorp. They're called Fragiles in our language. Well, some people call them that. I don't, of course."

"Of course." Was this what her mother had endured? Facing rejection from the Guardians and her own people over her choice of partner? Nadira sighed. "We didn't come here to hide, Jason."

"Your pardon, I did not mean to imply that," he gasped, genuinely alarmed at her response. "Jonathan is worthy of you if you have chosen him."

Chosen him? She wouldn't have put it quite that way. "Do you have any suggestions for finding Matt Bento's home?" she asked. "He recently acquired it from Novacorp."

"Really?" Jason's eyes grew wide. "That is quite unusual. They don't often sell property to a private owner. He must be a very wealthy individual."

"He is," Nadira replied. "And he does have company connections."

"If I could use my tablet, I might be able to find something."

"I'd rather you didn't. You've done enough to assist us."

"Then let me ask Lora. She might know about a house like that. That would certainly be something people would talk about." Jason rushed back to the house.

Four boats were out in the open sea, their blue and green sails puffed out by the wind. What if she just took a minute to slip out of her shoes and dig her toes into the sand? Just stand here and think about nothing more than the rush of water over her feet...like she used to do long ago.

The breeze was picking up. Nadira rolled down her shirtsleeves as she scanned the sapphire blue sea. Though right now the sky was clear, way off in the distance she saw streaks of dark grey clouds. A storm was coming.

But there was something wrong. She could feel it.

"AAAGGG!" Nadira pressed her hands against her head as a jolt of energy hit her, sending her down to her knees. She dug her fingers into the wet sand, steadying herself.

Another energy was bombarding her, striking at her vulnerability to force its way through. The shield she'd put around herself and Jonathan was crumbling.

Without the shield around him, any Guardian could track him. And when they found him...

She got back to her feet and ran down the path, ignoring the grass fronds that lashed at her legs. It didn't matter if Jon was still shutting her out. He'd have to let her shield him again.

Just as she reached the door, Jason appeared, sweat covering his ace. "Jonathan took one of the cycles! I tried to catch up with him, but he was moving too quickly. Can he drive them? Most people from the city are not good at handling vehicles."

Nadira groaned. Could he drive one? Probably not. But since when had that stopped him from doing anything. "Can a cycle move as fast as a transport?"

"Faster."

"Jason, I'm going to need your help again. We have to find Jon before he runs into trouble."

"If he doesn't have experience driving a cycle, he'll run into something else before then."

18 ARRIVAL

Nadira followed Jason back into the house, her nerve endings on fire. Why couldn't Jonathan stop and think for once? It was a good thing she'd been trained not to use her abilities in anger. Otherwise, Nadira was sure she would've blasted a hole in the wall.

"Lora!" Jason called. "Have the cycles been charged?"

She heard the sound of metal utensils hitting a hard surface, then silence. Lora came into the dining area, wiping her hands on her apron.

"No, Jare got backed up on other work and didn't get to it," she replied.

"That may be beneficial," Jason said, turning his attention to Nadira. "If the cycle isn't at full charge, it'll stop before Jonathan gets to the end of the transport road."

"How far is it?"

"It's about 70 kilometers to the end. After that there's just a quarry and a shuttle station."

"Shuttle? Of course!" Ilana was waiting for someone to come in on the shuttle. Nadira had thought she'd meant the shuttle from Nova City, but it had to be this one. "I didn't know there was a shuttle station here."

"It's used mostly by the quarry and the manufacturing plants to transport goods to the company installations."

"Matt's house must be nearby," Nadira observed. Now it made sense for Ilana and Matt to leave the city and come out here.

"Lora, tell Nadira about the house," Jason requested. "It might be the one she's looking for."

"I heard a house near the end of the transport road was sold by Novacorp," Lora said.

"No, that can't be it," Jason said. "You're thinking of the one damaged in the storm."

Lora shoved her hands into the pockets of her apron. "No, you're thinking of the house with the new manager. Remember, I told you I heard about the sale at the com station."

"Ah yes. They brought someone in from the city. What do they know about managing a house?"

"Not that one," Lora countered. "I'm talking about the one down the beach."

"I thought you said the new manager was at the one on the hill."

Nadira sighed. At this rate, they'd be discussing local gossip for the next hour. She was about to interrupt when she heard a low whirring sound coming from outside.

Whirrrrrr

"What is that?" She bolted out the front door, her feet barely touching the front steps as she landed on the sand-covered path. Directly across from her, a long, black aircar was hovering over the information kiosk. Oval-shaped, with a smoke-colored glass top, it resembled an oversized insect.

A breeze off the water whipped her hair against her face. Nadira pulled strands away from her eyes, squinting as she watched the craft's descent. If it was security, she and Jon were in a lot of trouble.

Jason came trudging out after her. "It's too large for a private vehicle," he remarked. "Do you think they're Guardians?"

After it set down, one of the doors lifted up like the wing of a bird. A security officer climbed out first, followed by a woman in a dark brown jacket and pants. Even from this distance, Nadira could tell who it was. Zina strode over to the information kiosk, the officer at her heels. It must've been her energy that had forced its way through Nadira's shields.

"Jason, I've got to catch up with Jonathan. Do you have another cycle?"

He looked at her warily. "Can you manage it?"

"I'll have to. That woman is a Guardian. If she questions you, just be truthful." Nadira darted back inside, grabbed her jacket and ran out the rear door.

Out back, the two remaining cycles were parked next to the transport. With all the shrubbery giving her cover, she should be able to get on the road without being seen.

"Should I tell her anything she asks?" Jason rubbed his hand across his balding head.

"Don't resist. She'll know if you're lying. The more you show your emotions, the easier it'll be for her to read you."

"Yes, I know," Jason said. "I have dealt with Guardians before."

"Thank you for all your help." She climbed into the cycle. The display lit up as the glass cockpit top came down and clicked into place.

If Jonathan could drive a cycle without knowing how, she certainly could.

"Use a light touch on the steerer--and be careful!"

She grabbed the u-shaped steerer, and the cycle lurched forward, accelerating with a press of her fingertips. Moments later she was speeding down the transport road, putting distance between herself and Zina.

Everything flew by in a blur as Jon sped along the transport road. Along the shoulder, all he could see was a ripple of beach grass waving pink, purple and green.

He'd had every intention of walking back to the com station. But the cycle, sitting there with the sunlight glistening off the shiny gold and black exterior, had been too tempting to resist.

Distracted by a large, black aircar whizzing by, he lost control as he rounded a sharp curve. The cycle swerved off the edge of the road. He mowed down a row of grass fronds, as the metal wheels screeched against the sand-covered shoulder.

His heart racing, he yanked the steerer to the left and wrenched the vehicle back onto the paved road. Shit. At this speed, he'd get back to the com station in no time. He'd just have to make sure he got there in one piece.

"Charge depleting in 10, 9, 8..." stated a tinny, feminine voice.

It was running down already? He'd only been riding for 15 minutes. Squeezing on the steerer didn't help, and neither did pushing any of the control buttons.

With a heavy sigh, Jon steered the vehicle over to the side of the road as it decelerated.

"3...2...1...charge depleted. Please proceed to a charging station within 10 minutes for a warm restart."

Well, back to the original plan. He climbed out and started walking. There was a beach house up ahead.

Maybe he could find someone to ask for directions. Picking his way through the grass, he headed down the hill and onto a gravel path.

"Pardon me." A slim man about Jon's age and height, called out from the gardens. "You're with the company, aren't you? Are you lost?"

"My cycle powered down. It's up there." Jon pointed up the hill. "I was on my way to the com station."

The man rushed over, his heavy shoes crunching against the gravel. "My name is, Corin. Would you like to come inside? It's cooler. Or maybe I can get you something to drink?" Rolling down his shirtsleeves, he wiped his hands against his long, blue apron.

"No thanks. Is this your house?"

"No. I'm the gardener." He wiped away sweat with his arm. "You passed the turnoff for the com station. It's about 16 kilometers back."

Damn it. "Do you know Matt Bento? I'm looking for his house.""

"I've never heard of him. Does he live on this end of the beach?" Corin asked, waving away an insect. "Most houses over here are owned by the company."

"He recently bought it from Novacorp. It's a big house overlooking the sea."

"Oh, yes, I heard about a house being sold. He must be very wealthy." Corin remarked. "If it's the one I'm thinking of, it's about a 20-minute walk. Or maybe 30 minutes. Sorry, I don't get down there too often."

"That's not too far. Thanks for your help," Jonathan said. If he was forced to wander around out here, at least he had something to go on.

"If you like, I could try to contact them and let them know you're coming."

"No, don't bother," Jon replied. "I'd rather it be a surprise."

Back on the road, Jonathan closed the cycle's cockpit. Grey clouds were gathering out over the water, and the wind was picking up.

Just what he needed, to be stuck in the middle of nowhere in a storm. He could always go back and take Corin up on his offer. A cool drink would go down great right now.

No, that would have to wait. There was important business waiting for him to take care of.

A buzzing sound from off in the distance caught his attention. Thunder? No, it didn't sound like it. It was more like a swarm of insects. What the hell?

Shading his eyes, he looked down the road. A cycle came into view, speeding in his direction. Was it going to stop? Jon dashed over onto the sand-covered shoulder, getting out of the way before the cycle whizzed past.

But instead of continuing down the road, it came to an abrupt stop, the metal wheels sending sparks flying.

Who the hell was driving that thing? The idiot could've run him over. He ran over to the vehicle just as the top lifted up and revealed who it was.

Nadira stepped out, brushing herself off as she glared at him.

"Can't you drive?" he demanded, as he slammed the top down. "You could've hit me."

"If you were in the medi-evac, at least I'd know where the hell you were!" She smoothed her hair back. "Why did you take off like that?"

"You know why!" he roared. "You should've trusted me. I had a right to know what happened to my father."

Damn, she was exasperating. Even now, he was having trouble resisting her. Pings of energy hit him like sparks, firing up his desire for her.

"Stop that. You're doing that Guardian thing again." He took a step back, retreating as she moved closer.

"Jon, you kept saying we were connected. Well, now we are. Do you think you can just walk away from that?" Nadira's words tumbled out. "You're right, I didn't trust you. I thought you'd go rushing off and do something stupid."

She had only been trying to shield him. He knew that. But still, he wasn't ready to reconnect with her yet. Not completely.

Yes, she was powerful, but he wasn't going to be overwhelmed by her or anyone else.

"You really think I'd do something stupid?" He ignored her dismissive eye roll. "Now that you're here, do you have a plan?"

"You took off in a cycle with no idea where you were going, and you want to know if I have a plan?"

She had a point.

"Look, I think I know where Matt's place is. It's about 20 minutes down by the end of the road," Jon said. "Think we could both fit in your cycle?"

"It's just about out of power. We'll have to walk. But we'd better hurry. Zina's here." Nadira closed her jacket and brushed off the sleeves. "Her aircar landed across from Jason's house."

"Then we'd better get going," he said. "I'll fill you in on the way."

Now that Zina was here, they'd have to hurry. One thing he knew for sure, she wasn't going to stop until she found them.

19 SHELTER

"We need to walk down there closer to the beach. The trees will give us cover and it won't be easy to spot us from an aircar," Nadira suggested.

"We'll have to leave the cycles here," Jon said.

They headed down the hill to the sand. Nadira threaded her way through the sea grass shoots, careful not to lose her footing. Jonathan raced down, not stopping until he reached the water's edge where he dodged a wave that splashed up and washed over his boots.

"I thought you didn't like the beach." Nadira joined him, suppressing a laugh as he stamped his feet in the wet sand, his pants bottoms sticking to him.

"I don't." Jonathan hunched his shoulders against the breeze that whipped up around them. "It's windy over here."

The clouds were quickly closing in; the bright sunlight giving way to a grayish sky and darkened clouds over the sea.

At least the aircar couldn't take off if a storm was coming. But the real problem was she and Jonathan would be caught out in it.

After about 15 minutes of travelling, Nadira was starting to miss the comforts of living in climate-controlled Nova City. Grey, purple-streaked clouds covered the sky, and a gusting wind pushed her with every step.

Deeply rooted in the sand, the gnarled trees that grew close to the water's edge shuddered in the wind. Their brownish-green bark was riddled with holes, as though they'd been chiseled with a miner's tool.

"The sea is getting rougher." Jon observed, as the foamy water crashed onto the shore, each wave rolling up higher than the last. "We should go back to the road."

"Being out in the open will be worse. We'll need shelter until it passes." At least there were a couple of houses up ahead. Hopefully the occupants were as friendly as Jason had been.

"Let's keep going a little more," Jon replied. "Matt's has to be close."

By now Jon's shirt was sticking to him, revealing the outline of his muscular chest. Even his curly hair was limp, with wet strands sticking to his forehead.

"Where's your jacket?" she asked, squinting to keep the sand out of her eyes.

"Left it back in the transport."

Her own jacket was damp and barely enough to protect her from the cooling temperatures. And the water kept washing up over her shoes.

The roar of the waves barreling in made it difficult to talk without yelling. Ducking her head to shield her face from the sand, she could barely see where she was walking.

"Jon, the weather's getting worse," Nadira said, raising her voice to be heard above the wind. "We'll have to get indoors until it passes."

"You're right. This is too much," Jon grabbed her arm to steady her. "Let's check this house coming up."

Stooping under a twisted tree limb, Nadira led the way over to a two-level, boxy house. It resembled Jason's, only this one didn't look as well kept. The window next to the sand-battered front door had a broken pane, and the stairs creaked as Nadira stepped on them. When she touched the rusted fingerpad, nothing happened.

"The windows are covered. Maybe it's abandoned," Jon offered. "Come on. We'll check the next one."

At least the next house was only steps away. Jon ran up and touched the fingerpad. The door creaked open. "Hello!" he called out.

She followed him into a large, empty living area that was lit only by the grayish light from outside. The air was stale, and smelled of salt water and something sour.

"It looks empty," Nadira said. In fact, it didn't feel like anyone had been here for a very long time.

There was a table large enough to seat four and an equal number of chairs scattered around. A puddle of water was spreading across the tiled floor, growing with each drip that fell from the ceiling.

"I'll check upstairs," Jonathan said.

Nadira walked through the open doorway that led to the kitchen. It was empty, except for some instant food packs that were on the counter next to the deep, stone sink.

She examined one of them. Fish soup, not exactly appetizing. It was enough to make her miss Jason's cheerful house. Back in the dining room, she peeled off her damp jacket and draped it over the back of a chair.

Rain pelted the window, leaving streaks across the glass. Zina wouldn't be a threat while this kept up.

A boom of thunder shook the house, echoing through the empty room. "Jon?" she called out. No answer. "Jonathan!"

Her response was a thud, followed by another one. Nadira rushed up the stairs. Breathless, she checked the first room. It was empty except for a chair facing the window. Darting to the room across from it, she got there in time to see Jonathan wrapping a blanket around him, his boots on the floor.

"What's wrong?" he asked.

"Why didn't you answer?"

"My shirt's wet. Figured this was warmer." He climbed on the bed. "Worried about me?"

"No!" He was the most exasperating man she'd ever met. "You like taking your clothes off, don't you?"

"I thought you liked to see me naked." He chuckled. "But I still have my pants on."

Nadira sat down on the edge of the bed, her back to him. Kicking off her shoes, she drew her legs up and sat cross-legged. Though she could feel a desire to be closer to him, she pushed it away. She was not going to give him the satisfaction.

Outside the wind continued to howl, whistling through cracks in the window.

"So, Zina can track me now?" Jonathan asked.

"Yes," she replied. "If she gets hold of you, she'll take you in and force you to tell her whatever she wants to know. And I'll probably be sitting in a detention cell next to you."

"Then we'll have to find Matt before she finds us."

Was he serious? "You make it sound so easy." Her back was aching. She inched up the bed and leaned against the headboard, leaving room between herself and Jonathan.

Clumps of sand hit the windows, as the wind continued to pummel the house. Considering the hole that was already in the roof, she hoped the house was strong enough to withstand the storm.

"Wonder if there's any confirmation yet about...my father." Jonathan stretched out his legs, his bare feet poking out from under the covers.

"Did Chief Mantee say why there was a delay?"

Jon snorted. "She was too busy being pissed at me. Cat saw Ilana's name on the shuttle passenger list."

"Wait." Nadira shifted so she could look at him. "She said she saw Ilana's name? How could she? Ilana used an alias. Remember?"

Jonathan's mouth gaped as her words registered. "Cat knew that Cintra Ansi was Ilana Travac."

"Only the Guardians knew about the connection, Jon. That information wasn't shared."

"Damn it, I should've known. I should've figured it out the way Cat was acting." He thumped his fist down on the bed. "That's why she didn't want me to get involved. She was in it with Ilana."

"Jon, don't." She grasped his hand. Through their connection, his energy rushed into her, like water breaking out of a dam. Quickly, she worked to put up her internal protections.

Her body shuddering as she fought to maintain control. She'd have to learn to manage it or before long she wouldn't be able to separate his emotions from her own.

"What is it?" he asked, cupping her chin in his hand. "What happened?"

"Our connection happened." Nadira sighed.

Jon wrapped his arms around her, his fingers caressing her back. Leaning against him, she felt the vibration of his steady heartbeat.

"Then it's still as strong as it was?" he asked.

"Yes."

As she'd feared, though she'd tried to maintain her personal protections, the connection between them had become permanent.

Jonathan pulled away, and before she realized what he'd done, he was straddling her. Holding her face, he kissed her, easing his tongue into her mouth with one firm stroke. He squeezed her arms, pulling her towards him.

She shivered at his touch. Getting up on her knees, she slid her arms around him, gliding her hands over his bare skin.

"Whatever happens, we'll get through it together," he whispered. "Do you trust me?"

"I should ask you the same thing," she replied, reaching up to brush a lock of hair off his forehead.

A smile spread across his face, his grey eyes filled with amusement. "I asked you first."

Running. He was running through the twisting tunnels that led deeper into the mine. And yet his pursuer was still behind him. Jon didn't know where he was going as he dashed through the damp, hollowed out caverns.

Rocks moved beneath his feet. Another step would send him tumbling over the edge of a precipice. Digging his fingers into the openings of the slick, machine-blasted walls, he groped his way back from the edge...

"Jonathan! Wake up, Jon." A soft voice echoed through the darkness. Calling him back.

His eyes snapped open as he gasped for air. "What? Where am I?"

Nadira was kneeling on the bed in front of him, her gold-flecked, brown eyes shimmering. "You were dreaming. The storm's over. We have to go."

He sat up and ran his hand through his hair. "How long was I asleep?" A dream? It felt real, right down to the dust he still tasted in his mouth. But why would he dream about being in the mines?

"Almost an hour. I was talking to you and all I heard was a snore." She eased off the bed.

"I don't snore." Stretching, he joined Nadira at the window.

The sea was back to its regular sapphire blue calm, the waves gently lapping onto the shore. Even the dark clouds were gone, with just a few smudges of red, gold and purple against the horizon.

"It's almost sundown. We'd better get going," she said, as she rolled her shirtsleeves down.

"Too bad I didn't stay awake." Jon pulled his boots on. "We could've done something else to pass the time."

She narrowed her eyes at him, the hint of a smile on her lips. "We didn't have time for that."

"There's always time for that," he replied, slipping into his shirt.

"Jonathan, you are just--"

Whirrrrrrr

"Damn it! What's that noise?" From deep inside he felt a vibration scraping his nerve endings. Wincing, he ran to the window.

There was nothing out there but a flock of brown birds gliding across the water.

"I don't hear anything," Nadira said, as she reached out to him.

Jon rushed out of the room and was halfway down the stairs before he heard Nadira's footsteps behind him. The door swung open and he bolted out onto the sand.

"Jonathan!" Nadira grasping at him, trying to catch hold. "What is it?"

A black aircar was slowly heading in their direction. It was hovering lower to the ground than usual, probably scanning the area as it travelled.

"It's Zina. Hurry, Jon you have to go find Matt's house. It can't be much further now. I'll get her to stop."

"No," Jonathan said. "We're going together." He wasn't leaving her to face her mentor alone.

"I can delay her. If you stay, she'll take you in. Please go ahead. I'll catch up."

Her tone was insistent, but he wasn't having it. "I'm not going without you."

"Jonathan, don't argue!" Nadira clutched his arm.

"She's tracking me, right? We'll lead her right to Ilana and Matt."

"And what if we can't find the house v ? she asked.

"Look it's landing." He pointed to the aircar as it descended. "It must be setting down in that open field on the other side of the road."

"If Zina picked up your energy trail, she'll track you to this house," Nadira said.

"Staying on the beach will slow us down." Bits of grass, tree bark and driftwood were scattered across the beachfront. "The road would be better."

"But we'll be out in the open."

"I know." He sighed. "Okay, we'll stay on the beach for a while. Matt's house has to be close by. It won't be long now."

"All right. Let's go," she said.

Jonathan took her hand and they headed down the beach.

Nadira looked back at the distance they'd covered. It had to be almost two kilometers by now. At least the trees were thicker on this part of the beach, obscuring them from anyone who might be following.

Up ahead, the beach ended at a cluster of jagged rocks that jutted out into the sea.

On this part of the shore, the sand was lighter and shimmered in the late day sun. Speckles of light grey mixed with beige and even bits of pink, like someone had taken a basket of crystals and emptied them out along the shore.

"Damn," Jon said, gripping one of the tree limbs, "we can't get through this."

He was right. Here there were no houses filled with staff to trim back the growths. So the trees grew wild, their limbs twisting, bending and linking together, forming an impenetrable living wall that stopped them from travelling any farther.

"You're right. Let's get back on the road." Nadira said.

A narrow gravel path led them away from the beachfront. Here the grass was growing just as wild as the trees, with fronds shooting up past her knees. A few of the taller shoots lashed at her arms, stinging her through her thin shirt.

The hill was steeper here, and the sand-covered incline made it difficult to get her footing.

"Get hold of the stems," Jon suggested, as he grabbed a bunch of fronds. "Pull yourself up."

Following his lead, she did so, managing to haul herself up the hill and onto the road. Jon climbed up after, but not without yanking out a handful of the shoots.

"At least that grass is good for something." He threw them on the ground and wiped off his hands.

Nadira brushed off bits of fuzz as she scanned their surroundings. So far so good. No aircars, no security and no Zina.

"What's that? I think I see a building behind those trees," Jon said.

Across from them, set back from the road, stood a grove of trees. These weren't bent and twisted like the ones along the shore, but standing erect, their limbs shooting straight up and loaded with small red thorns. Beyond them she caught a glimpse of a large, slate grey house.

"That looks too big to be a house," she said. "Maybe it's the shuttle station."

"No, that wouldn't be over here. Where would they take off from?"

"Let's check it out."

She kept her awareness open as she weaved in between the trees. A place like this had to have a security force.

"Look at that," Jon said.

Balconies stretched across each of the four levels, each with a set of glass double doors. The windows flanking the front door were two-stories high and were trimmed in gold. In fact, all the trimmings were gold, even the pointed spires that capped the corners of the house. No one could mistake it for just another Novacorp standard-issue seaside home.

"Who are you and what do you want?"

Nadira turned to see a security guard approaching. Dressed in a one-piece, dark grey uniform, her face was partially obscured by a shiny helmet. As the guard got closer, she realized the oval-shaped object in her hand was a stunner.

She'd allowed herself to become so distracted, she hadn't sensed the guard's presence.

"We're looking for Matt Bento," Nadira replied. "Is this his house?"

"Yes. Where did you come from?"

With a quick glance at Nadira, Jon responded. "We're with the company. I'm Jonathan Keel. This is my associate. We're expected."

After what they'd been through, both of them probably looked like they'd washed up on the beach. Reading her emotions, Nadira could tell that the woman wasn't sure, but didn't see them as a threat.

The guard lowered her weapon. "We'll see about that. Come with me."

20 HOMECOMING

Walking into Matt's house was like walking through the Nova City shuttle terminal--oversized and overwhelming. All around him, Jon saw signs of Matt's enormous wealth on display. From the jewel-encrusted, pink marble floor, to the gold railing across the upstairs landing, to the matching marble staircases that led to the second level.

"What the hell is this?" Jon asked, as Nadira joined him in the middle of the entrance foyer.

"It makes the Emerald Club look like a mining installation," she replied, staring up at the clear glass roof.

"This way." The guard motioned to a set of open double doors on the left. "Wait in Mr. Bento's office."

Jon entered the room, his feet cushioned by a furry white carpet. Matching chairs and couches trimmed in gold were placed around the room. Matt's gold-trimmed, black desk sat opposite the door.

"Jonathan!" Matt rushed into the room. "What are you doing here?" He motioned for the guard to leave them.

Jon was shocked at how terrible Matt looked. His grey hair hung, scraggly and greasy. His dark red shirt was stained on the front, possibly from sweat or having something thrown on him, and his pants were ripped at the knee.

"Matt? What happened to you?"

"Why did you come here?" Matt's eyes were glassy. "You have to leave now!"

"Where's Ilana? Why are you protecting her?" Jon asked.

"I have to, Jon. or she'll turn me in. I'm not going back to the mines."

"Going back? But you worked in the mines--didn't you?"

"I was sentenced. Five years for embezzlement." Matt staggered over to one of the plush couches and fell back on the cushions. "When I was released, I met your father and Catherine. We worked together here on Hathor. Your mother and I were friends too, Jon. And I wanted her to--"

"Matt. That's enough."

What the hell? Jonathan spun around. Standing in the doorway was his father, Brandon. Wearing a dark blue pullover jacket and matching coveralls, he looked more like a miner than an executive.

"Dad!" In two long strides, Jon was gathered into his father's embrace. "Cat told me you'd been killed in the explosion!"

Brandon pulled back, his powerful hands gripping his son's shoulders. "They found me in one of the caverns a couple of days ago."

"But why didn't Cat tell me?" Jonathan asked. As usual, his father's chin was covered with short stubble, but a long, thin scar on the left side of his face was red and blistered.

"She had her reasons. And this is the Guardian who's been protecting you?" He extended his hand in greeting. "Thank you for protecting my son."

"Dad, this is Nadira. She was investigating the robbery."

"How did you get here so quickly?" Nadira asked, as she shook Brandon's hand.

"The freight shuttle from Demeter is faster," Brandon said. "Son, when you called Catherine earlier, we were on our way here. She couldn't tell you the truth."

"Cat is here too? Where is she?" Jonathan asked.

"Upstairs with Ilana. They had some business."

"If you had settled it sooner, we wouldn't be in this shit." Matt sneered.

Brandon gave him a look of disgust. "You've made your share of mistakes. And that's why we're here."

"Jonathan, I have to talk to Ilana," Nadira said. "There's something wrong. I can feel it."

"I'll come with you," he replied.

"No. I'll be all right. I'm prepared for her this time."

Jonathan waited until he heard her going up the stairs, then turned back to his father. "When I called Cat, she knew Nadira was with me. She wouldn't tell me how, but it makes sense now. Matt told her. Dad, what are you all involved in?"

"Well, let's see...I've violated about four or five Novacorp directives...and if security finds me here with the..." Brandon shoved his hands into his jacket pockets. "It'll be enough to condemn me to hard labor in the mines."

"You're not the only one who'll be going," Matt grumbled.

Jonathan felt like he'd just been punched in the gut. "Tell me what's going on."

Brandon sighed. "All right. I'll explain it to you."

Nadira found Ilana in one of the upstairs bedrooms. All the furnishings were gold, down to the tables and chairs. The room practically glowed in the light of the setting sun, the red-gold rays flooding through the two oversized windows. Over the bed hung a huge mirror fitted into a thick, wooden frame.

Lying on the bed, Ilana seemed dwarfed by her ornate surroundings. Her dark hair pulled back from her face. With no trace of makeup, she looked washed out and much younger than Nadira remembered. Threads stuck out where her shirt was ripped at the shoulder. Ilana gripped the handle of a small, black case sitting on the bed next to her.

"Who are you?" A short, trim woman jumped up from her chair next to the door, her blonde hair cropped close to her scalp. Her green, company-issued jacket had the half-moon Novacorp logo and "Security Chief Mantee" stamped on the front.

"My name is Nadira. I'm a Guardian."

"Show me your hands," she ordered.

Nadira complied. "You're the one who brought the payment, aren't you?"

"It's right here." Ilana patted the case.

Giving the woman a look that was sharp enough to cut through stone, Mantee whipped out her stunner. "You're lucky I don't use this. If I'd known you were at the mine, I would've."

"I want to speak to Ilana alone."

She pocketed her stunner, her blue eyes like frost. "Why? What are you two up to?"

"It's not your concern," Nadira snapped.

The Chief's eyes narrowed, her hand still in her pocket. Her energy flared, hitting Nadira's awareness like hot sparks off a drill. Casting a glance at the woman reclining on the bed, Mantee walked past Nadira, making sure to leave enough space to avoid touching her.

Ilana's forced laugh echoed through the oversized room. "Well, at least I'm not the only one she hates."

"Jonathan, I'm sorry for putting you through this." He motioned for them to sit on one of the couches in front of Matt's imposing, stone desk. "You have every right to be angry."

"What about Mother and the girls?"

"Your mother knows all about it." As he pressed his fingers against his temple, Jon concentrated on the tongues of flame tats encircling his father's wrist. Mining was his life, but he'd been ready to throw it all away for what?

Cat ran into the room. "That Guardian is upstairs with llana. Who knows what they're planning."

"Go to hell, Cat," Jonathan snapped. "You don't know what you're talking about."

"Give me a reason to blast your ass." She whipped out the stunner and waved it in his face. "I should've done it before you left Astarte."

Brandon held up his hand. "Can the two of you please stop bickering?"

"Dad, there's not much time. I'm being tracked by another Guardian. You've got to tell me what's going on."

"Are you serious?" Cat asked. "Why didn't you tell us when you first walked in?"

"There's an alert out for me. I tried to tell you, but you were so pissed about Ilana you weren't listening. We saw the aircar a couple of kilometers back. It won't be long before they track me here."

Brandon looked over at Matt, who was staring straight ahead, oblivious to the activity around him. "Catherine, go find that security guard. Tell her to call out the rest of them so they can patrol the grounds."

"And then what? We're talking about company security here. They'll blow this place apart if they have to," she protested.

"I know that. Just do it!"

21 CONTROL

"What do you want? Revenge for what I did to you?" Ilana rasped. "I've used up my energy. Do it and get it over with."

"Show me your hand."

A grimace passed over Ilana's features. "I'm not a Guardian, but I still have this." Keeping her right hand on the case, she showed Nadira her left palm.

"Guardians don't use their powers against each other." Nadira sat on the edge of the bed. "Who trained you?"

"No one."

"Don't lie to me." Ilana energy was waning, but she still had enough to keep Nadira from reading her. It was like trying to see though a granite wall. There was no way around it or through it.

"I'm from the West. My abilities didn't develop until ten years ago, when I was 18." Ilana settled back against the headboard. "My family wanted me to use my power for their profit. When I refused, they threw me out. I had no where else to go, so I went to Nova City."

"To find the Guardians?"

"No. I never wanted this power. I wanted to hide it. In the city, I thought no one would be able to tell. But I was wrong." Sighing, she wiped her eyes. "When I got there I had no credits. No place to stay and no family. Finally, I got work at a meet up club."

"A meet up--what were you doing there?"

The clubs were filled with workers hired to entertain wealthy executives and businesspeople. Some worked there by choice and others out of necessity.

"Are you sure you want to know?" Ilana asked. "I was nonahli. So, I did what I had to do."

Nonahli. Without family or shelter. An outcast.

It was a word Nadira hadn't heard in many years.

"I was involved in...an altercation. One of the execs tried to force me to do something and I refused. He ended up in a medi-evac and I was thrown into detention." She wiped away a tear with the back of her hand. "They discovered I had abilities and contacted Zina. She got me out and told me I'd be trained as a Guardian."

"Zina? But your powers are strong, Ilana. She would've been bound to have you brought before the Elders. It's required."

"Required." Ilana laughed. "You are very naïve. Do you think the Guardians never put self interest first?"

"We have a duty." It was what she was brought up on, from her first days of training.

"When Zina found out I wasn't a Sentry, she had no interest in training me. She already has you. With two Sentries, she'd have leverage over the Elders. Instead she had me track Matt Bento. She suspected he was stealing from the company. My job was to get proof. But, as it turns out I found out much more than that." She patted the case.

"She's the one who gave you the company ID," Nadira said.

"She didn't mind breaking a few rules to do it. But she wanted to catch Matt herself. Novacorp would reward her and the Guardians would have to give her a place with the Elders," Ilana said.

"Did you report back to Zina?"

"When I found out what Matt and Keel were doing, it gave me control over the wealthiest man in Nova City and the CEO of the richest mine in the system. Why share that with Zina? But Keel wouldn't give me what I wanted, so I had to show him I was serious."

"How did you leave Hathor. No one with abilities can leave."

"Do you still believe that old story?"

"Answer my question," Nadira said. She wanted the truth. And yet, she didn't want it.

Isn't it time you stopped believing everything the company tells you?" Ilana shook her head.

"You're lying." Swallowing, she tried to ignore the pounding in her chest. Stay calm. Don't react.

"You know it's not a lie, Nadira. Admit it," Ilana said, a faint smile on her lips. "It's what you've been told to keep you from leaving the planet. Haven't you ever wondered if it was really true?"

Yes, she had wondered. But she'd forced it from her thoughts. If it was true, she and her mother could've escaped. Shaking, she fought to contain the feelings exploding inside her. An image of her mother formed in her mind. She was crying as Nadira was pulled away.

"I don't want to hear anymore!" She jumped up and blasted the mirror over the bed. It flew across the room and smashed against the wall. Her chest heaving, Nadira fell to her knees. They could've left Hathor together and been safe.

"Now you know how it feels," Ilana said, her voice just above a whisper. "To be powerful and powerless."

"Nadira! What's going on up there?" Jonathan called out.

She pulled herself back up and wiped the tears from her face. When she got to the doorway, Jonathan was halfway up the stairs, his face flushed.

"It's all right." She folded her arms across her chest, as she tried to stop her body from shaking. "Nothing's wrong."

He didn't move. "Come downstairs with me."

"Not yet. I'll be down in a few minutes."

"Are you crying? What did she do?"

"Jon, please."

He turned, as if in slow motion and headed back downstairs.

She had to pull herself together. Now. There was work to do and she couldn't let her emotions get in the way. Dropping her arms to her sides, she walked back into the bedroom.

"What did you mean you had to show Brandon Keel you were serious?" Nadira asked.

"You recovered quickly," Ilana smirked. "But you have to in your position as the all-powerful Sentry."

"You robbed the mine for someone. Was it Keel? Is your payment in that case?"

"That's why she took you from your mother, isn't it?" Ilana asked.

"What are you talking about?"

"Zina told me about it. When she discovered how strong your powers were, she destroyed your entire family to get to you." Ilana lips twisted into a cruel smile. "Oh, that's right, Zina was your mother's cousin. That's why Guardians renounce their families once they're trained. No feelings about anything but duty. I feel sorry for you."

DEBORAH A BAILEY

Gritting her teeth, Nadira held back a wave of re-vulsion that threatened to engulf her. She wasn't going to be baited into reacting again. "Zina's on her way here."

"Good. As soon as my energy is fully restored, I'm leaving Hathor. I was going to contact Zina and tell her everything once I was far away from this planet. But this will be better. I'll be here to see Keel and the others dragged off to detention in restraints."

Nadira lunged across the bed, grabbing Ilana by her shirt and yanking her up. "You're not going anywhere!"

"The company will put them all in the mines. What do you care?" Ilana grabbed Nadira's wrists. "You think Jonathan cares about you? Do you know how the company execs use us?"

"Why did he pay you?" Nadira wrenched herself out of Ilana's grasp.

"Just like your mother, there are many people who'd rather leave Hathor than turn their children over to the Guardians. Keel helps get them off world on the shuttle to Demeter. From there, they can go wherever they want." Ilana sat up on the bed, her voice gathering strength." Matt's in it too. So is that bitch, Mantee."

"How much does Keel get from the families?"

"Nothing. Can you believe it?" Ilana leaned back and closed her eyes. "He paid me with crystal from the mine so I wouldn't expose them. If the company finds out, they'll seize all his assets and throw him in the mines for life."

The crystal and Ilana's testimony would be proof of Brandon's involvement. CEO or not, he'd be punished. But how could Zina cover her own duplicity with Ilana? She was in violation herself.

"You said you have the power. Then why would you help Zina? Instead of training you to be a Guardian, she used you for her own gain," Nadira said.

"Everyone uses everyone else, don't they? Novacorp runs this world, Nadira. We belong to them. And when Jonathan tires of you, you'll find that out."

22 SHATTERED

"What's going on up there?" Brandon asked as Jon came back into the office. "Ilana's not to be trusted."

"Nadira can handle it," Jonathan said.

"When we got here she'd drained her power. She and Matt had a fight."

Matt was still sitting on the couch, but now he had a drink in one hand and a half-empty decanter in the other. Maybe he was better off.

His father had admitted to taking crystal to pay Ilana, and he'd explained about helping people leave Hathor. Other than that, all he'd done was apologize for putting him in danger. But yet, he still wasn't telling Jon the one thing he wanted to know. Why?

"Son, the shuttle for Demeter will be leaving in about a half hour. We have to get to the station."

"Dad, I told you, I'm not leaving Nadira here. Her mentor will throw her into detention for helping me. You and Cat go on."

"I'm not leaving without you. That's why I came here," Brandon said.

"You still haven't told me your reasons for going against company rules. I mean, I know forcing people to be Guardians is wrong, but what's that got to do with you?" Seeing where it had gotten them, it didn't make sense. Why would he take such a risk?

"Jonathan?" Nadira walked in. "You've all got to get out of here. before Zina comes."

"No," Jonathan said. "I'm not going without you."

Nadira addressed Brandon. "The Hathor Novacorp Guardian Agreement states that anyone who tampers with citizens under the protection of the Guardians or who have been identified as candidates for training, will be detained. It doesn't have to be proven. Being suspected of such activity is enough. Do you understand?"

"What are you talking about? Are you detaining him?" Jon stepped between her and his father.

"No, Jonathan. But when Zina gets here, that's what will happen. Ilana is going to tell her everything."

"Son, that's why Cat falsified the report about the remains. She wanted you to stop looking for me and come home. When the Guardians found out you brought Ilana here, they started asking questions."

"How could you trust her?"

"I didn't. But she was good at getting Matt's confidence. He told her things he shouldn't have. Years ago, he wouldn't have made that kind of mistake."

"Brandon, their meeting wasn't accidental. Ilana works for Zina," Nadira said.

Jonathan felt like his heart had dropped to his feet. Ilana had the payment and the proof. It wouldn't even matter if they left now. As soon as Zina found out, the company would send security after them.

"Then she's been reporting back all along," Brandon said.

"No, she hasn't. Not yet."

"Dad, why did you do it? Was it worth it?"

"Yes, damn it! It was worth it." He sat down, his shoulders slumped. "Years ago I was an independent miner here. Catherine and I met up in the West. We did mining, excavating, whatever we could get."

"That's why you don't have an ID chip, isn't it?" Nadira asked.

He pulled back his sleeve to show her the tongues of flame tat that circled his wrist. "I prefer these. Novacorp didn't force the issue. My mine is a top producer." Brandon rolled his sleeve back down. "I met Jon's mother, Estrella when I was 23 and she was 17. Her family was in business selling mining equipment. That's how we got to know them."

"Wait a minute," Jon interrupted. "I thought you two met on Astarte."

"We never told you the entire story. After about a year Estrella started developing abilities. Out there, we thought she'd be safe from detection. Guardians usually stuck to the North when they were hunting. But, her powers got stronger and...well...one day two Guardians showed up. They said someone contacted the District Manager's office about her. It could've been anyone who worked with her family or maybe one of her relatives. I don't know."

"It happens," Nadira said. "Neighbors, friends or family will report it."

"Guardians help protect Novacorp's assets, which makes them very valuable. And Estrella's abilities were strong. She would get visions and was able to touch objects and see who had owned them. I didn't understand it very well. It was tough for her to experience these things and not know how to deal with it."

"What happened?" Nadira asked.

"After her abilities developed, we discovered she was pregnant. If they took her away, I'd never see her again. And we didn't know what they'd do about the pregnancy. She didn't want to be taken by the Guardians and she couldn't get clearance from the company to leave the planet. So, Catherine and I hid her on an equipment shuttle bound for Demeter. From there, we travelled to Astarte."

Jonathan couldn't believe what he was hearing. This had to be a story his father was making up. "I don't get it. Why didn't you tell us?"

"We didn't want to take the chance the company would find out. It was best if you and the girls didn't know anything."

What else didn't he know? Were there any other secrets? "Does she still have those powers?"

"No, Jon." He looked at Nadira. "I know Novacorp tells you that you'll die if you leave here. It's not true. Once you leave Hathor, your abilities will fade over time. But that's it."

"I know," Nadira said, her voice shaky. "Ilana already told me."

"She did? What did she say?" Jonathan asked.

"What happened when the Guardians came to get Estrella?" Nadira asked, ignoring Jon's question. "Did they detain her family?"

"No," Brandon replied. "Her mother told them Estrella had been killed in a mining accident."

"And they believed it?" she asked.

Brandon looked down at the floor. "She wasn't on Hathor and they couldn't track her. I wasn't with Novacorp back then, so once I left no one was looking for me. I was just another miner who came and went. But she can't ever come back here, or see her family or communicate with them. She had to disappear. That's why we're not contracted. Neither she or my daughters are listed in the company records."

"But why am I listed as your son?" Jon asked. "Why me and not the girls?" Remembering the anxiety in his mother's eyes when he'd talked about coming to Hathor, he realized now why she'd been so upset.

"I accessed the company database to add you when I took over as CEO of the mine. I'd hoped one day you'd want to work with me and possibly take over the management. That's why I added your name to the records. Novacorp doesn't recognize unions unless there's a company-validated contract. That's why I wasn't required to add your mother's name."

His mother had escaped from Hathor and could've become a Guardian. Within minutes, Jon's entire world had shifted.

"I would've lost everything if they'd taken her away," Brandon said. "After I took over the mine, I got word from Estrella's mother. There were others who wanted to leave Hathor. I helped them. No one should be forced into a life they don't want. I don't care if they think having abilities is a gift. It's not."

Jon continued to watch Nadira for any signs of what she was feeling about this. Her expression was unreadable, and her emotions were locked down. She just stood there, refusing to meet his eyes.

Across the room Matt was drinking out of the decanter now, the empty glass on the table next to him. Had he helped out of loyalty to an old friend?

But Jonathan didn't get the chance to dwell on it because in the next instant, the world around him exploded.

The window shattered, sending glass flying in every direction. Jon dropped to the floor, pulling Nadira down with him.

"There's an aircar out there on the transport road! It's firing on the house!" Cat screamed from the foyer. "Get out here now!"

23 PAYBACK

Jonathan scrambled to his feet, pulling Nadira up with him. Jagged shards of glass were sticking out of the window frame. Outside he could make out movement as guards scrambled across the grounds.

"Let's go," Brandon said as he hustled them out of the room.

Cat dodged three guards as they ran past her, heading out the front door. "Brandon. We waited too long. We have to get out of here now."

"What the hell is going on?" Matt bellowed, still clutching the liquor decanter. "They have no right to do this."

"Zina must've had a security detail with her," Nadira said.

"Son, take Nadira and go out the back. There's a path leading to the shuttle station down the road."

"No, Dad. I'm not leaving without you."

"Jonathan!" He clutched his son's shoulder. "It doesn't matter. When they come here, they'll find out what I've done. I can't run away from it."

"Brandon, the Guardians don't know that you and Chief Mantee are here. If you leave now, I can protect you," Nadira said. "They won't be able to track you."

"What can you do?" Cat asked, her tone skeptical.

"When Ilana tells them what I've done, it won't matter."

"I'll make sure that Ilana's not a threat. Think of your family. If you're detained, everything will be revealed. They'll force Estrella back here," Nadira argued. "You have to go now."

Jonathan gazed into his father's eyes. He saw the worry and the pain. If there was a chance, his father had to take it. "Dad, you have to trust Nadira."

"All right," Brandon agreed.

"We'll go out the back. Come on!" Cat grabbed Brandon's arm and led him to the rear of the foyer.

"What about Ilana? Are you going to be able to stop her?" Jon asked.

Nadira nodded. "I'm going to try."

"What are they doing out there? Get away from my house!" Matt rushed out the front door.

"Matt!" Jonathan grabbed at him, but missed.

"Never mind him, Jon. Come with me." Nadira led him to the room across from the office. This one also had large windows, and gold furnishings. It was a mirror image of the office, except without the oversized desk. Nadira sat on the nearest couch.

Jonathan sat beside her. "What now?"

She grasped his hands. "I'm going to shield your father and Chief Mantee. But I'll need your help."

"You've got it."

It was just as he'd felt when she'd protected him before. The familiar tingling spread across his body as her energy flowed through him. He allowed his own energy to flow into it, creating the foundation, constructing the shield that would keep his father and Cat from Zina's detection.

Nadira willed herself to tune out the noises that surrounded her. Footsteps thumped across the marble foyer, accompanied with shouted orders from Matt's guards. Jon's energy supported her as she shielded Brandon and Chief Mantee.

"Where are you? This is all your fault!"

The window behind Nadira shattered into thousands of fragments, spewing shards of glass across the room.

"What the hell?" Jonathan threw himself across her. His body protecting her as another window blew out.

Stunner fire echoed across the grounds, followed by the sound of a scream.

"Jon, what's going on?" Nadira sat up, but found that Jonathan was refusing to let her sit up.

"Stay down. Someone's firing into the house." He lowered his head as a stunner discharge lit up the room. "We've got to get clear."

He pulled her to her feet and rushed her towards the door. But just as they got there, she saw Ilana speeding down the stairs. Clutching the case, she was heading for the front door.

"You're not going anywhere!" Nadira sent out a blast that hit Ilana and knocked her into the wall. The case flew out of her hand, landing in the middle of the foyer. Ilana slid down on the floor.

Jon dashed over and grabbed the case. "I'll take that."

Ilana narrowed her eyes at Nadira. "You don't learn do you?" Struggling to her feet, she fell back against the wall again, her chest heaving.

"Where are you going?" Nadira asked. By not using her full strength, she'd avoided the rebound of energy. She'd have to hold on for a little while longer. Maintain her shields and keep from draining herself.

Matt staggered back into the house, his scraggly grey hair hanging across his face. "J--Jon what are you doing with that?" He pointed to the case.

"What's wrong with you? You're an idiot!" Ilana rushed towards Matt, her arms outstretched.

Matt dodged her and ran into his office, followed by Ilana right on his heels.

"Come on!" Nadira followed them. Jonathan right behind her.

"No! Don't! Stop it!" Matt cried out as Ilana reached up and grasped Matt by the throat. They both fell back on the floor. Ilana straddled him, gripping Matt's neck as she banged his head against the carpet.

"Matt!" Jonathan lunched for her, grabbing her shoulders, trying to pull her off the older man. ""You'll kill him!"

Jon pried Ilana's fingers off and the force sent him on his back, his hands gripping her wrists. They rolled across the carpet, and against the side of the couch.

The influx of emotions hit Nadira, making her head spin so much that she could barely stay on her feet. Her adrenaline pumping, she fell back against the door and braced herself. Ilana was regaining her strength and Nadira had to stop her before she could focus her energy.

Matt was on his hands and knees, coughing so much that he sounded like he was about to vomit. His body heaved as he grabbed a chair and pulled himself up.

Another stunner blast shot through the open window, illuminating the shards of glass that still hung from the frame. Wincing as the whine of the discharge cut through the air, Nadira ran over to where Jon and Ilana were wrestling. Ilana working to free herself from his grip, and Jon refusing to let go.

"Jonathan! Let her go!" Nadira called out. "Let her go!"

But he wasn't focused on her and he continued to struggle as Ilana kicked him.

"Stay back, Nadira! Damn it!" Jonathan rolled her onto her stomach, pressing her into the carpet as she continued to buck.

"Jon, let her go!"

"What?" Jon asked, glaring at her.

The distraction was enough to give Ilana the advantage. Wrenching one of her hands free, she reached back and touched Jonathan's leg.

"Yes, Jon, let me go!" Ilana mocked.

"AAAAGG!" Jonathan released her and fell back on the floor, his body trembling.

Ilana fell back and braced herself against the couch, kicking him as he writhed in pain.

Nadira's emotions surged through her as she focused her energy and threw out a blast.

Ilana screamed as it hit her hard enough to send her somersaulting over. Gripping her fingers into the carpet, she wrenched herself up.

Nadira felt her preparing for another energy blast. If she could get Nadira to spend her own energy, Ilana could overwhelm her.

Several of Matt's guards ran through the foyer, their boots tramping against the hard marble floor. Nadira jumped back as the discharge from one of their weapons ricocheted.

In that instant, Ilana ran past her and out of the office.

"We have to get out of here!" Jonathan got to his feet, and joined Nadira at the door. "Zina must've called an entire security team."

"I know." Nadira's struggled to catch her breath. "Jon, we can't let Ilana go."

"Then let's get her."

"No, stay here with Matt." He was leaning against the couch, his eyes closed. "I'll get her."

She ran out into the foyer, avoiding three more guards who shoved past her on their way through.

Crunching on bits of glass and splintered wood, Nadira followed them out the back. The glass double doors leading outside were now just empty frames.

Outside overturned tables and chairs littered the stone patio. In front of her, a gravel path led through a grove of trees similar to the ones out front. She couldn't see what was back there, but she could make out lights in the distance.

"You haven't had enough!" Ilana screamed, running towards her. She reached out her hand and sent out an energy blast.

Where had she been hiding? Nadira dodged out of the way, rolling against the stone floor. As she came to a stop, she sent out a blast in return.

It hit Ilana in the chest and sent her smashing against the doorframe. She slid down to the floor with a groan.

As Nadira came to her feet, she heard more stunner fire and the sound of heavy footsteps inside the house. It sounded like several people were running up the stairs.

Just as she reached the doorway, two people walked out onto the patio.

"Jon!" She ran over to him, then stopped when she saw who was behind him holding a stunner.

"You have betrayed us, Nadira." Zina walked out, her weapon pointed at Jonathan. "And now you will pay for your mistake."

Every nerve ending in Jonathan's body was tingling, and every instinct called for him to grab Zina's weapon and tear it out of her hands. He knew that was a crazy idea--suicidal even--but he couldn't let her hurt Nadira anymore. Whatever she was planning, he had to stop her.

Nadira's eyes were locked with his. Too bad he couldn't tell what she was thinking right now.

"Ilana, that is a fitting place for you," Zina said.

With a slight turn of his head he was able to see Ilana on the floor. She eased herself up, leaning against the wall for support. "You've always looked down on me. But when you wanted to use me, it was different, wasn't it?"

"She told me what you did," Nadira advanced. "It was a violation to use Ilana without going through the Elders. You'll be punished."

Jonathan felt movement behind him. Was Zina about to blast him? If he could turn around and grab her before she realized what he was going to do...

"I suggest you don't try it, Mr. Keel," Zina said.

She'd read him. Damn it. His thoughts were exposed to her. He had to be careful in case he put Nadira in danger.

Nadira darted her eyes to the right. It was a small movement, and he barely caught it. Clearing his mind, he took a deep breath and hit the floor, rolling to the right and away from Zina's line of fire.

When he looked up, Nadira was raising her arms towards her mentor, her body rigid.

The energy blast hit Zina and sent her back against the broken door. She fell against it, grabbing hold of the frame to stay on her feet. Her weapon flew across the patio. Before Jon could react, Ilana scrambled over, picked up the stunner and aimed it at Zina.

"I should've done this long ago." Ilana aimed the weapon, her finger pressing against the firing button.

Zina lunged at her and grabbed Ilana's wrist. They fell against one of the overturned tables, and the weapon fell from Ilana's grasp. Zina grabbed it, pointed it at Ilana, and fired.

"Zina!" Nadira cried out.

A blast of bluish-white light, hit Ilana in the chest. There was no scream, or even a sound from her. Instead she rolled down on the floor as the discharge reverberated through the air.

Jonathan ran towards her and stopped. Ilana was lying at Zina's feet, her eyes open, a sizzling hole in her chest. Jon fought back the urge to vomit as the smell of smoldering flesh filled his nostrils.

When Zina faced him, she was breathing hard, her mouth half open.

"You killed her!" Nadira screamed.

"The Guardians must be protected, Nadira." Zina lowered the weapon, her hand shaking.

"You did it to protect yourself! She told me everything!"

"You've never understood the danger we face! If we show any weakness, Novacorp will use it to destroy us. Ilana was a thief and a killer. I had to do it."

"And you're no different than she was," Jonathan said, unable to take his eyes from the dead woman lying on the floor next to him.

"Enough! Mr. Keel you're coming with me," Zina said.

"Now I know why you were looking for Jonathan. You wanted to know if Ilana had told him about your plan. You were afraid that if he knew, he might tell Matt Bento that you'd sent Ilana to investigate him. You had no authorization from the Elders or Novacorp and you didn't want that to come out. You put out the alerts and chased us here to cover up your wrong-doing."

"Where did you hear such a story? From that slag?" She motioned to Ilana's body. "You believe her over me?"

"Zina, all you've ever wanted was power. That's why you destroyed our family and killed Ilana. No wonder you're an empath. You suck the life out of everything you touch!"

"How dare you address me in that way." Zina raised her weapon again. "I trained you! If it wasn't for me, you wouldn't be a Sentry. Obey me or accept the consequences."

Jonathan moved in between Zina and Nadira. "Put that weapon down," he ordered.

He felt Nadira's grip on his arm, but he wasn't going to move out of the way. Zina would not get the chance to do to Nadira what she'd done to Ilana. She'd have to go through him first.

She laughed. "And what will you do about it?"

"This," Nadira replied.

"Noooo!" Zina's scream pierced the air.

Dropping the weapon on the floor, she staggered back. Groaning like an animal trying to free itself from a trap, she pressed her hands against her head.

Next to him Nadira's breathing was rough and her hand shook as she continued to grasp his arm. She wasn't blasting Zina as he'd seen her do to others, but she was sending out a lot of energy. Grunting, he shuddered as the rebound sent a shower of pinpricks through his body.

By now, Zina was clinging to the doorframe, her body heaving.

"Guardian, I--" A security officer walked out and froze when he saw Zina slumped against the door. He pulled out his weapon. "You attacked her!"

"Escort her back to the aircar," Nadira said, showing him her palm. "Do it now."

"Guardian! Yes, I--I will." Reluctant to touch her, he stood back as Zina straightened up. Without a backward glance, she staggered inside, the officer a few steps behind.

"What the hell did you do?" Jonathan asked as he took Nadira into his arms.

She sagged against him. "I flooded her with my emotions. That's why you felt the rebound."

"Are you all right?"

"Yes, I'm fine," Nadira said. "She knows that if she tries to go against me, I'll tell the Elders what she did to Ilana. She'll either be forced to leave Hathor forever or sent to detention. Sending her to solitary would destroy her. She needs to feed off the emotions of others."

"She'll leave us alone then."

"Ilana was apprehended. The company will be satisfied with that. They won't care how it happened or why. Where's the case?"

"Back in Matt's office. When Zina walked in, she asked where you were. Then she pointed that stunner at me. She didn't even notice the case."

"Then we can return it to your father."

"Were you able to keep your protection around them?"

"They've left Hathor, Jon. No Guardian can track them now."

"Does that mean it's over?" he asked.

"Yes, Jon. It's over."

24 Epilogue

Three Days Later

Nadira sat at the counter in the dining area of her apartment. She stared into her half-finished cup of tea as she reviewed the events of the past few days.

Exhausted after their return from the North Country, she and Jon had collapsed in bed and stayed there. Drained of energy, she'd slept for an entire day. After two days of doing little more than eating and sleeping, she felt her energy coming back again.

The shower door opened and Jon stepped out, a towel around his neck.. "That felt good." He approached her and slid his arm around her back, leaning close to kiss her cheek.

"Jon, you're going to wet me up. Why don't you use your towel?"

"If you had a dryer you wouldn't need towels." He rubbed his face against hers.

Feeling his stubble against her face was strangely stimulating, but she wasn't in the mood for anything more right now. "I like using them. Besides, this is an old apartment. I don't have all the luxuries you're used to."

"A body dryer isn't a luxury," he said, running his hands over her bare arms. "You don't have to stay here, you know. We can get a place in the Palatine district."

"Jon, let's take it a step at a time. I'm comfortable here. Besides, you'll be going to Astarte soon."

"Only to visit." He hugged her, planting a big kiss on her neck. "And maybe you'll come with me."

"We'll see." She glanced in his direction in time to see his bare bottom disappear around the corner as he headed towards the bedroom. That was another topic they'd have to discuss. Though she could leave Hathor, it wasn't easy to accept something she'd been told all her life was impossible.

If only her mother had known, that one fact would've changed her entire life.

At least Brandon and Catherine Mantee had managed to escape without detection. Jonathan had been visibly relieved when his father had contacted him from Demeter.

One day they'd have to confront the truth about Jonathan's origins. If he started to develop abilities, what then? And what of Zina's actions? She'd taken a life. It didn't matter that Ilana wasn't a Guardian.

She'd have to check the company records and see if she could find anything about Ilana. Was her story true? It was plausible. But Zina would never admit to it.

Stifling a yawn, she set the cup on the counter. Used to waking early, she'd wanted to get up at 5:00 this morning. But Jonathan didn't see the point of rising before sunrise.

He'd convinced her to stay in bed and snuggle under the covers. Of course, it hadn't taken much convincing on his part.

Jonathan came out of the bedroom and stood in front of her. He was wearing a pull-on blue shirt that fit close to his body, and dark pants that fit rather well in other places. Grinning, he turned around to model for her.

"How do I look?"

"You already know the answer." She smirked.

"Be back soon." He kissed her.

"Jon," she said. "I can go with you."

Matt had been taken to the medi-evac after he'd been detained by company security. But after about a day of medical observation, they'd shipped him off to detention building. Whether he'd be sent back to the mines or released hadn't been determined yet.

His wealth could go a long way towards getting people to forget about his connection to Ilana. Since she could no longer tell her side of things, she'd get all the blame for the robbery.

"It's better if I go alone. I won't be long."

"All right." She wasn't going to force the issue. But she could see that he was going to continue being stubborn about some things.

He went to the door and paused before he touched the fingerpad. "By the way, I'm stubborn about a lot of things."

"Hey! You said you couldn't always tell what I was thinking."

"Not always. Just enough to keep things interesting."

The detention area was so different from the rest of the city that Jonathan was almost reluctant to get out of the transport. It looked desolate, without color or any activity other than the movement of security officers. Nadira had requested that he be given access to talk to Matt, and thanks to her he didn't have to pass through the regular checkpoints. Instead, he'd met the chief of security for the detention complex, and she'd personally escorted him to Matt's lockup.

"How long will he be here?" Jon asked, as they walked down a long, brightly lit corridor.

"That depends. The decision will come from company administration. They questioned him earlier. If he doesn't go back to the mines, he'll have to leave the planet for a while. Maybe forever."

At the end of the corridor, Jon had to pass through a set of double doors, then a single door that pulled back into a pocket in the wall. Inside there was a small space, just large enough for one person.

Matt was dressed in the grey knit top and pants, just like the clothing Nadira had given Jon after his attack. There was just a chair, a bed and a combination toilet/wash area in the corner. Up near the ceiling a small window provided a slit of sunlight that reflected off the shiny, metal surfaces.

"Jonathan. I didn't expect you to come here." Matt stood, his hand gripping the edge of the chair.

"How are you, Matt?"

"Better." He dropped back down in the seat. "I almost didn't make it."

Jon perched himself on the edge of the bed. The cushions weren't soft, but they were functional.

"I need to know. What happened? How did you let Ilana do that to you?"

"You should know the answer to that. She knew how to find your vulnerability and exploit it. Isn't that how she got you to bring her here?" Matt replied.

"Why did she need to come back here? Why didn't she just go to Cat and get her payment while she was on Astarte?"

Matt shook his head. "She needed to get back here to regain her power. If they stay away from Hathor too long, they lose it."

"You were suspected of stealing from Novacorp."

"I'm not. It was a set up."

Jonathan expected him to say more, but instead he looked down at his folded hands. Matt looked years older than he did just days ago. He had dark circles under his eyes and creases cut into his forehead. He already looked like he'd been living in an underground cavern for years.

"You let her attack me and Nadira. She'd already attacked my father at the mine."

"When I called you, I didn't know she was going to be at my apartment. She came after I talked to you."

"But you knew she sent those men to kill me."

"No, they were supposed to take you from the hotel. That's all. Besides, I didn't know anything until after she set it up. I never meant anything to happen to you." Matt rubbed his hands over his face.

"Why did you tell her about my father getting people off Hathor?"

"I thought I could trust her, but it was all a lie."

"My family trusted you. How could you betray us?"

"Betray? That's funny, Jon," Matt snorted. "Ask your father about betrayal. When we were all working together years ago in the West, your father betrayed me. He knew how I felt about your mother. He knew it and he took her away from me. And you know why he did that? Because she was pregnant with you. Her family wanted to get her away. But you know the real reason? They wanted her with your father because he was successful and had everything I didn't have."

Jonathan fought to hold back his rising emotions before he did something he would regret.

"Are you saying that Brandon's not my father?" Jonathan slammed his hand on the bunk. "Damn it, answer me!"

"You're his son, all right. You're both just alike," Matt spat. "I'd been sentenced to the mines. Brandon was successful and growing wealthy by then. He talked her into staying with him after she escaped from Hathor. She believed Brandon could protect her from the company if anyone found out the truth. But I didn't have influence then. I had nothing.

Matt pulled back the grey hair that hung down on the left side of his face, revealing the tat that was placed on all thieves who were sent to the mines. Resembling two interlocking chains, it was branded a centimeter or two from his ear.

"Matt!" Jonathan had never seen this before. His father's friend had, as long as he'd known him, worn his hair long, covering the sides of his face.

How could he have known this man all of his life, and never known this?

"I could have the mining tats removed, but not this. It's a reminder."

"If you're angry at my father, why did you help him?"

"I did it for your mother. I thought one day, she'd realize what I felt for her. I have as much wealth as your father now, if not more. I thought she'd see that I'm the one who really loved her." He buried his face in his hands.

Even though he didn't have her side of the story, he knew Matt was lying. His mother hadn't stayed with his father because she'd been forced to or because of his wealth. They were in love and that was something Matt would never understand.

"You did it for yourself, Matt. You and your exec friends were stealing from the company. Ilana was going to tell the Guardians. You told her about my father to save yourself. And you know what? When you did that, you also put my mother and sisters in danger. Got anything to say about that?"

Matt waved him off. "You need to go now."

"You're right. There's nothing else to say."

When Jon returned to Nadira's apartment a couple of hours later, she was anxious to hear what had happened.

"What did Matt say?"

"Do you think he'll get sent back to the mines?"

"I don't know, Jon. If he gets protection from his friends, who knows? The company might not want his punishment to become public knowledge, considering how prominent he is. It won't reflect well on Novacorp."

"So they'd rather hide it?"

"If others see what he could get away with, then it will be known that the company is vulnerable. They'd rather make this go away."

"Is that why Zina's getting away with it?"

"If I tell the Elders what Zina did, the rest of the story might come out too. Your father will be sent to the mines. Is that what you want?"

"It's not right. My mother can never see her family again. Hell, I can't even meet them."

"You can't take the chance, Jon. Anyone who knew about it or helped her to escape will be sent to detention, or worse. Your family will be forced back to Hathor. If your sisters don't develop abilities, they'll be nonahli. Outcast with no family or friends. Forced to survive any way they can. You must never forget what's at stake."

Jonathan sat down next to her on the couch. "It's still not right."

"That's how it has to be for now."

He wanted things to be resolved and the guilty to be punished. So did she. But it was going to take a while.

"Jon, why don't we go out? Let's go back to the plaza."

"Since when do you want to go out in a crowd?"

"Let's get away from here for a while and not think about any of this." So much had happened over the past few days. She wanted to clear her mind of it all. If just for a few hours.

"All right," Jonathan said. "Let's go."

After dinner they strolled over to the waterfront and sat on a metal bench facing the water. It was quieter here. Off in the distance, a ferry boat skimmed across the water, lights blazing. Above them, the moon Isis followed Osiris across the starry night sky.

"I've been meaning to ask you, why is your club called, 'The Answer?'"

Jonathan smiled, remembering why he'd chosen it. "My father always wanted me to follow him into the mining business. When I got the club, it was my answer. After that, Dad realized I wanted something different for my life."

He slid his arm around her shoulders and felt her warm energy flowing into him. At the time, his club had been the answer. But now, everything was different. Hathor was where he wanted to be, and it was where he wanted to stay.

"Yes, you can stay, Jon," Nadira said.

"What? Oh, so you can read my thoughts too?"

"Jonathan, really, I've always been able to do that," she said, laugher in her voice. "But I promise not to do it all the time. Just enough to keep things interesting."

ABOUT THE AUTHOR

Deborah A Bailey's other published works include a short story collection, Electric Dreams: Seven Futuristic Tales, two non-fiction books, and articles for various online publications.

Visit http://www.BrightStreetBooks.com/ to learn more about her current books, find out what she's working on, and see what's coming next.

www.ingramcontent.com/pod-product-compliance
Lightning Source LLC
Chambersburg PA
CBHW061559170626
46811CB00001B/258